COTTONMOUTH KISSES

CLINT CATALYST

MANIC D PRESS
SAN FRANCISCO

To my parents,

for giving me life, unconditional love and support

To Anne Barrows, Adam Klein, and Aaron Shurin,

for teaching me the urgency of life

Massive gratitude/thanks to Almighty HP, Ayofemi Folayan and Word!Architecture students, AK, Sham, Samuel Anthony Hunt, Daniel Cartier, Dawn Tlusty and Dylan, Stanis, Roman Chimienti, Shawni and X, Nakako, Lake Vajra, Lakey and Co., Thomas Roche, Debbie Finley, Marjorie Lingenfelter, Hope Norman Coulter, Mira Kopell, Jack Butler, Bryan Rabin, Jayson Elliot, Matt, Anna Noelle Rockwell, Kim and John, Todd Hughes and P. David Ebersole, Dvd, Bill Mills, Maria, Angelyne, Molly McGee, Steve Diet Goedde, Yvette, Monique Motil, Jade, Hannah, Brant Mayfield, ★BOB★, Gabriele, Hallie Goodman, Sweet P., Desireé, Kimberly Burks, Allen Siu, Lolia, friends of Dorothy and friends of Bill, Tobi, Heidi, Lara and Alicia Vanian, Amber Gray, Apollo Starr, Ayn Imperato, Benjamin, Brandon Taylor, Cat and Tom @ Carpe Noctem, Charles Gatewood, Colin and Candice, Stephen Lee, Dharma, Dayve Morffy, Elizabeth, Terrance, Erin, Felix, Garland Richard Kyle, Michelle Tea, Blair Murphy and Videssa, Katherine Ramsland, Lynda Licina, Mary Woronov, Jerry Stahl, Keith Border, Poppy Z. Brite, Miss Lynda, Adrienne, Tina Root, Susan Wallace, Amy, Liz, Carol, Tim, Michele Mills, Mick Mercer, Lee, David and Co., Jenny Roberts, Autumn, Omewenne, Danielle (wherever she may be), Lara Haynes, Machiko Saito, Maendi, Nick Bohn, Pauley Perrette, Ru, T.L. and Miguel, Tony Havoc, Spencer Distraction, Dennis Cooper, Iris Berry, Gothic.Net, Luie, Steven, Tim Van Deusen, Craig Chester, and of course, Jennifer Joseph and Manic D Press, without whom this would not have been possible.

Cover photo: Stephen Lee   Cover design: Scott Idleman/Blink

Some of this work originally appeared in *The Anatomy of Melancholy, As If, Bathory Palace, Belief of Strangers, Black Lotus, Black Moon, Danse Macabre, Dark Angel, The Darkside, Dragstrip, Elegia, Ghastly, Gothic.Net, Graceless Passion, Greetings From Sodom, Impetus, IndustrialNation, in remembrance, Levity, Machine Gun Etiquette, The Magic Mountain, Morbid Outlook, Necropolis, Nocturnal Images, The Ninth Wave, Notre Sagesse, Oblivion, Potpourri, Permission, Premonition, Praxxis, Psychodaisy Anthology, Reflections: A Poetry Quarterly, The Rift, Rouge Et Noir, Suffering is Hip, Soul Manifest, Screem, Subnormal, Tear Down the Sky, Theatre ov the Night, Thoroughly Queer, Tractor Press: Mid-South Poetry Journal, Twilight, Virtute et Morte, Xian Angst,* and the forthcoming anthology *Noirotica 3.* Thanks to the editors.

Library of Congress Cataloging-in-Publication Data

Catalyst, Clint, 1971-

Cottonmouth kisses / Clint Catalyst.
        p. cm.
     ISBN 0-916397-65-3 (alk. paper)
     1. Goth culture (Subculture)--Literary collections. 2. Drug abuse--Literary collections. 3. Gay youth--Literary collections. I. Title.
     PS3553.A81927 C38 2000
     818'.609--dc21

                                00-009002

CONTENTS

The water moccasin, or cottonmouth, *Agkistrodon piscivoris*, is a venomous snake – one of the few poisonous snakes in North America. The bite of the cottonmouth is highly dangerous, and may be fatal. Its fangs are like hollow hypodermic needles, which inject poison into the victim's body. Its threatening posture, with head lifted and chiseled jaws agape, reveals the white lining of the mouth – hence the name 'cottonmouth.'

CARESSES SOFT AS SANDPAPER

SOME NEW KiND OF kick

The X begins to hit me, tingle in my groin, inner thighs.

Ten after eleven and I'm leaning against the sheetrock of my usual Saturday night spot, the right-hand wall of Lillith's dance floor. Silhouettes of dark figures sway in the fog of the room, the features of nearby dancers discernible in the faint red overhead lights.

The club's actually attractive tonight. Reminds me of the way it seemed when I started coming here around a year back, the excitement I got from observing impeccably dressed people before I could predict their outfits, the rush I got from listening to mysterious music before it became routine. As the bass of "Love's Secret Domain" by Coil vibrates the room's foundation, seeps into my skin as if it were liquid static, this place seems new to me again. Magic.

And big fucking deal if it's drug induced. Jeffrey gave me the hit over a month ago, but I didn't take it till tonight, didn't resort to chemical happiness till I got bummed-out because Sean flaked on plans to go out with me around half an hour beyond the last possible minute, or however the expression goes. Responded to my two reminder messages with an abrupt "Can't make it," no explanation given, no chance for me to question, line chopped off the second syllable of a generic "later." I'd actually looked forward to seeing him. Must be a payback for something.

Whatever. I'd already gotten dressed, which is why I ended up here anyway, date or no date. Wouldn't want to waste a complete outfit, even if I'm basically bored with the scene at Lillith's. Wouldn't want to waste a dose of X, especially if it could make the old dive interesting.

I close my eyes and feel the touch of light to my eyelids, the caress of cigarette smoke to my cheeks. Ah, I could really get into a cigarette.

Even better, a clove. I can tell this is good X, because I never crave cigarettes, don't even like to be near them. And Sean had said the batch of X circulating now is bunk! *Damn* was he wrong. I feel myself sifting into the wall, the back of my knees and shoulderblades turning to warm water.

Open eyes and there's a sea of phosphorescent splotches, glowing white painted faces, dark makeup around the eyes. Now the club is full of its regulars, dance floor packed with night's creatures, people lined up on either side of me. The room has come alive in no time, and I'm drenched in its electric energy, eager for something to happen. Ready to walk away from the wall and the chubby punk girl on my left who's sloshing beer with loud gulps. Ready for excitement, adventure like I used to have, instead of the ennui my life has become. Ready for some new kind of kick.

"Skin and Lye" by Malign starts up, Xavier's voice full of fury, voice growling and screeching over ominous background music. The crowd on the floor dances slowly, writhing, sending ripples of movement into the audience gathered around them, tendrils of smoke twisting around safety-pinned jackets and teased hair.

I breathe in smells of leather and hairspray and cigarette smoke, a long slow breath, their scents filling my nostrils, settling on the back of my tongue. I smack my lips. The X has hit me full-force, and I am on fire.

I see two figures standing out from the others, standing out from old friends of mine, fucks, whatever. Two figures draped in velvety black material, hooded cloaks framing their delicate features, fragile-boned faces. Strands of raven hair spill 'round the edges of their slate-colored skin.

I can't tell if they're male or female or both or neither, but they're pressed close together, leaning against each other, shoulder to shoulder. Siamese twins with the exact same build, except that one stands a couple of inches taller than the other.

Who are they? I've never seen them before, but they're too perfect to be real, too lucid to be a dream. Somebody *new*! New, completely new and free of the "Oh, I've heard about you from so-and-so" garbage that's about as interesting as a soggy microwave pizza box lining.

Brow moist with sweat. My skin hot, alive. They're staring at me seductively, dusky eyes brazenly glowing, and I feel my blood rush. They're devouring me with their eyes.

I'm dying to speak with them, introduce myself, but I have no idea where to begin. Must be the drugs. They're beautiful, completely androgynous and alluring. How could I resist the opportunity to speak with a couple of people to whom it's obvious they can have anyone they want? It's been so long, so dreadfully long.

Dead Can Dance's "How Fortunate the Man with None" begins, and I feel Brendan Perry's smooth voice cover my limbs with a blanket of tingling sensations. The X is hitting me so hard, I'm on the verge of either exploding like a grenade or passing out. My eyelids flutter, the image of the duo blurry, the clusters of people in the room bleeding together into a smudge, like watercolors painted on a paper towel. I'm being reduced to the sway of the music.

"Hi." I hear a voice within earshot, and I open my eyes wide, focus. "I'm Byron."

Something twists inside my stomach. Now the erotic duo is directly in front of me, close enough to touch, the taller of the two extending a slender hand. *Byron.* So he's male. I place my palm within his, grasp it. Shudder at its warmth as he politely pulls it away.

"And I'm Gitane," a second voice adds, offers a hand of her own. My palm meets hers, rests against smooth skin. *Gitane.* A female. I examine her chest area as she retracts her hand, but none of her body shows through the material.

I study their faces, compare the similarities between their meticulously arched eyebrows, deep chocolate eyes, prominent cheekbones, well-formed noses, raspberry-stained lips. It's remarkable how closely they resemble one another, each a mirror image of the other's striking elegance.

It's impossible for me to speak, impossible for me to look away. The whole club has been shut out, and nothing but this sensual feast exists, my heart racing as I'm devoured by their ethereal presence and the refrain of "*The world however did not wait / But soon observed what followed on .*"

Byron and Gitane are statuesque, patiently awaiting my response.

"How Fortunate the Man with None" crescendoes, peaks with lavish strings and horns. Byron leans forward, centers his cool ivory face before mine, wraps his hand around my upper arm.

"With us," he says, face expressionless as he tightens his grip. "Now."

He positions himself between the punk girl and me, twists my arm like a slab of taffy as he scrapes me off the wall and slides behind me. Shoves my left hand up my spine, stops when my knuckles press between my collarbones. Steps forward, overtakes my balance, shoves me chest-first toward Gitane.

I stumble, feet sweeping the floor as he steps again, pushes me past Gitane, steps again, again. He weaves me through the mass of people standing around the dance floor, strands of their sticky hair brushing my forehead and cheeks, their sweat and perfumes stinging my eyes, dripping bitter taste between my lips as I try to cry for help. The weaving stops when we make it to a cluster of Goths and cyberpunks blocking the doorway marked with a flickering "HEAD" sign in blue neon letters. There's a split second pause; then he uses my upper torso to part the crowd, their shoulders and metal jacket adornments smashing against my ribs, shouts of "*Asshole!*" and "*What the fuck?*" following as he pushes me through the bathroom entrance.

The room is washed with dull yellow light. I feel my face squinch in disgust, the stench of piss and lemon air freshener filling my nostrils as I'm led toward the urinals. Byron moves up to the left side of me and reduces his grip on my arm, frees it from its locked position. It drops, dangles. Gitane files in on my right, the two of them leading our dance across the slippery tiles, the floor slick with toilet water and spilled beer. We slide past an empty stall with its door open, a closed door, a closed door, an open-doored stall with a leatherman hunched forward taking a piss. Then we make it to the last stall, where a generic-looking guy with a brown buzz cut is exiting. Gitane steps behind me, allows room for him to get around us. He does a double-take.

My feet slip as I'm shoved into the stall, but Gitane and Byron hold me up, prevent me from busting my ass on the floor. Byron slams the cubicle door shut, the sound of metal against metal echoing ominously. It fades, and muffled reverberations of Siouxsie and the Banshees' "Spellbound" remain.

"...*From the cradle bars / Comes a beckoning voice / It sends you spinning / You have no choice...*" Siouxsie's eerie voice still entrances me after all these years, voice rich with enchantment and disheartening splendor. "*...Following the footsteps of a ragdoll dance...*"

A flurry of hands unfasten my pants and tug them open, the air cool on my bare ass. Natural instinct overpowers drug euphoria, and I reach down to cover myself, suddenly aware what's happening.

"No!" Byron shoves me onto the toilet, my asscheeks slapping the porcelain seat.

"But I- but I-" I hear myself speak, but my words are high-pitched and pleading, sound foreign.

"But you *what?*" He grabs the bottom seam of my shirt and rips it to the collar with a single flick of the wrist, tatters the velvet into two pieces.

"I'll use you as much as I want, day or night, for as long as I want." He tears the remainder of the shirt off me, tosses it onto the floor, whacks me across the ear. A lightning bolt of pain cracks into my temples.

Oh my God, what have I gotten myself into? I look up at the two sets of eyes glaring at me and see a faint reflection of myself repeated across the four murky orbs, my pants wadded around the knees, private parts exposed, chest patterned with the fresh splotches of red and purple across it. I'm embarrassed at what I see, how I feel, vulnerable and afraid.

Byron leans forward and tenderly kisses me on the shoulder, his lips warm and smooth as liquid, hood tickling my jawline. "But you'll love it," he whispers against my neck, his voice deep and comforting.

I watch Gitane watch him lick a trail to my ear and flirtatiously flick the lobe, and I'm filled with a strange sensation of pleasure, a combination of submission and dominance and exhibitionism unlike anything I've experienced. Byron's hand moves up my thigh, and I'm scared, excited, my cock starting to rise.

Gitane unbuttons the neck of Byron's cloak and removes it from him, exposing the tight white skin underneath. She drapes it over the side of the stall and he moans into my ear, his hair tumbling down my back, his voice passionate as the sound of rustling velvet.

Gitane pulls at the neck of her own cloak and extracts it, exposing her small frame squeezed into black satin bustier. A boy, looks maybe sixteen or seventeen, must have borrowed the i.d. of an older brother or friend, opens the stall door halfway, tries to enter. The door bumps Gitane's back as she situates her cloak beside Byron's. She turns, notices his innocent face and laughs, her lips a violent red smile.

"Whoops! Guess we forgot to lock it," she says.

Boy takes a half-step back, blue eyes wide, disconcerted. Byron moves from me, pulls door rest of the way open. Grabs the boy by his shoulder, holds him in place.

"Well, hello," he says. "Watch."

Eyebrows raise in disbelief.

"Huh?"

Byron spreads my legs apart with his knees, pushes each to either wall of the stall. The metal partitions are cold. I flinch. Gitane pulls my head back by the hair above my neck, laughs again. My lips part and release a soft moan of embarrassment. She leans forward, positions hers around them and pulls back, strings of saliva snapping between us. They fall around my cock head, cling to it as if it were a maypole.

"I said *watch*."

Byron keeps one hand on the boy's shoulder, digs his fingertips into the flesh around the collarbone, extends his other arm to reach the half-hard bulge between my legs. He circles the head with index finger, smooths the spit into a ring. Spreads it down my cock. Forms a fist around it, pushes down. Pulls up. Pushes down.

"He likes this very much, see?" He says, third person, detached. Sneers with the crinkles 'round his eyes. "See the way his whole body moves with the rhythm of my hand?"

The boy doesn't answer, also doesn't look away. Stands there in a stupor of fear and awe. He looks vaguely familiar to me, though I don't know why. Stares at me with ice blue eyes, looks down at my dick, now fully erect. The excitement in his face crackles, pops like bacon fat.

Hand continues moving up and down my dick. I shut my eyes, moan.

Gitane scoops a breast out of her bustier, pushes two fingers between my lips, pries my mouth open, inserts nipple. I stroke it with my tongue, lap the salty sweet taste of her skin.

Open my eyes. She and Byron are violently kissing, lips pressed together, jaws in motion. Byron's eyes are also open. One of his hands still holds the boy in place, the other pumps my dick. He watches us, stops kissing her, smiles at me, takes his hand from my bulge. It bounces, rebounds from his touch. Throbs.

Slowly, delicately, he pushes away from me. Tugs on my bangs, forces my head upright. He unzips his tight pants and his cock falls out on its own, half-erect. Fingers run through my hair, Gitane's, Byron's. Pulls me closer. His dick is directly before me, its head large and light red.

"Come on," he says, his voice stern. "Suck it."

Split second longer of cock before my face; then disappears between my lips, into my mouth. Eyes close habitually. I take it all the way to the base, my nose buried in dark tuft of hair, his musky scent filling my nostrils.

"Yeah," he moans. "That's good."

And it is good. I love the way he feels in my mouth, the energy of his dick throbbing as he slides it against my tongue. Pulls himself out to the head. Pushes to the back of my throat.

I move my left hand between Gitane's silky thighs, nudge the strip of material covering her sex. Her clit is hard and slick. I rub my fingers against it, smear her wetness. Rub it harder, faster. Feel her thigh muscles tighten around my hand, her hips jerk.

I touch myself with my right hand, cock throbbing and burning. Thrust my forefinger deep into Gitane's wetness. Move my tongue against Byron's cock so slow it's barely moving.

Samples of bubbling water, hollow drumbeats, an angelic voice. Ambient dreamscapes of The Future Sound of London seep into the stall, accelerate our sensual energy.

Byron shudders, starts pumping furiously. Almost too much for me to handle. Tears form in my eyes as his dickhead bangs against the back of my throat, balls slap my chin. My lips make sloppy smacking noises against the base of his cock, and a small retching sound escapes from the back of my throat. I desperately gasp for air, but I love it.

He loves it, too. "Oh yeah," he says through clenched teeth. "Keep fuckin' blowing me. Suck me off, you little slut."

His deep voice intensifies my excitement. I stuff three fingers in Gitane, her inner lips hot and luscious. My dick drools, and I tighten my grip, pound in rhythm. Pound furiously.

I squeeze my tongue around his cock and look up, watch the muscles in his stomach tighten. Watch him groan as Gitane plays with his nipples. He thrusts his hips forward, greased cock rapidly gliding in and out of my mouth as he leans against the boy, cradles his arm around the adolescent neck.

The boy's eyes meet mine and a sharp rush of panic shoots through my chest. *Oh my God. Those eyes. I know those eyes.* Reminders of that glossy blue, that soft face, that scraggly bleach blond hair, the small silver hoop earring, swim from the depths of my memory, the inner recesses of my mind. *But it can't be, just can't be, they can't be.* My consciousness swirls.

I pull my hand from Gitane and long ribbons of wetness stretch down her slender legs, spill onto mine. Byron continues thrusting himself into my mouth with an increasing sense of urgency, groaning desperately, arm locked tight around the neck of the boy, standing solemnly, staring. *Those eyes. Those eyes.* Those eyes freeze my lips with a chill of horror, the edges of my teeth scraping Byron's skin as he gives himself a final shove in my mouth.

He pulls out and comes with an idle rush, sperm cascading from his cockhead and sticking onto my face and neck like ornaments, like quivering jewels. His discharge reeks of salt and soured milk. The small puddles collapse under their own weight and shimmy down my shoulderblades, my stomach, my shrivelled cock, in thin pasty trails.

There's a trace of gummed-up whiteness in my eyelashes, but I don't move to wipe it away, don't move whatsoever. The boy's lips unfold in a soft gesture that could be shock or disgust or pity, and it's astounding how much I know him, remember him.

Byron examines his midsection, yawns, flicks a stray pearl off his pisshead toward me. It spatters into my right eye, crude and merciless.

An acidic stinging stifles my vision, makes me wince. I frantically knead my aching lids with the jointed edge of a fist, but slender fingers scramble around my wrist, pull my arm away. Within seconds, the fingers find their way to my face and calmly move back and forth on both eyelids, producing tears that wash the stinging away. The fingers then move to my forehead, my cheeks, and sweep off small lumpy bits, smooth my skin to dry stickiness.

I blink until the blurry orb I see transforms into the young boy. It's the sandy-haired teenager who's comforting me, caring for me with his gentle touch, leaning forward into my muddled space, his azure eyes sparkling and curious.

He smells of soap. I recognize the vigorous rhythm of the Orbital's "Halycon and On and On," realize he's moving towards me.

He presses his lips to mine and gives me a rough kiss, a kiss of inexperience, tongue darting around in my mouth, scraping against the rawness in my throat. The kiss is uncomfortable and long. His tastebuds feel like dry gravel as he pushes his tongue farther into me, wiggles it. It's as if he's trying to reach all the way to my heart, yearns to lick my soul.

I clumsily wrestle with him, attempt to bulldoze his tongue back to its home, when suddenly it hits me: I taste myself in his mouth. I twist my tongue around his, taste the sweet nectar of summertime at my grandparents', taste the excitement I felt sneaking out of the house to smoke pot with my best friend, taste the swarm of adrenaline I had when I lost my virginity. I taste the richness of memories, and I want to tumble into them, wallow in their splendor.

The boy breaks our embrace, backs away from me with a grimace, leaves me panting, my torso quivering. Gitane and Byron have clothed themselves, and he clings to them, glares at me with glittery eyes.

My stomach grumbles. I'm hungry for that taste I found, crave it the way a dieter does chocolate. I know I can't have it; I know the boy tore himself from me because of the bitterness he discovered back in my spongy cave of a mouth, a bitterness toward life and humanity that tastes like poison to a boy whose innocence remains unmarred, whose romantic ideals still seem plausible.

The frantic way he clutches Gitane and Byron, small arms sunk elbow deep into their cloaks, tells me he's afraid my depravity will work its way into him like a virus. I'm sickened by the realization of what I am, this jaded monster I've become. But I wonder who Gitane and Byron are, why they've come to me, what they represent, what sort of lesson they're trying to teach.

Split second and they are gone, stall deserted, door gaping wide, stained grey concrete wall replacing the line of vision where they were. I try to call after the boy, call my name, but it catches like a cinderblock in my throat. *His name, my name. He who I used to be.*

Tears blossom and flow like blood as I sit in this stall, frail and slump-shouldered, wishing I could return to the face that once was my cradle, my home.

ACTIONS SPEAK

Sunlight
Slithering through the curtains
Signals an end to our warfare:
Conflict finally finalized, complete.
I unlace my arms from around you,
Examine the stripes on your back
Where fingers have been,
Swab them with my tongue,
Stare at my reflection
Delicately gleaming
In small puddles of sweat and blood and spit,
Unravel strands of flesh from
Beneath my nails
and push myself out of bed,
Each of my movements magnified:
Actions speak
              and loud

ONLY PICTURES

I've only seen pictures of
Goya's painting *Saturn Devouring*
One of His Children, only seen
Flat reproductions in books

Copies less detailed, small versions
Of that break from the grandeur of myth
I long to see in its original glory,
Long to plunge my fingertips
Into the mucous mirage,

Those dark grooves of oil, that image of Saturn
With his knuckles sunk into the rubbery spine
Of a torso frail and flaccid and bare,
Saturn's eyes shiny and swollen as insect eggs
About to hatch new lives but

His face filled with terror
And his mouth filled with blood while
He sucks on a stump where once was the head
Of his child now dormant, devoured, dead

I, too, by this portrait often fall prey
And am slaughtered by the thought
Of knowing deceit instead of truth.
This falsehood I can't bear. I want to be

Right there, examining each streak
Of Goya's graffiti, right there
Among the stains
As real and living as flesh

Where I will press my lips against
The stain among that skin of a canvas,
Smother Saturn, suck the marrow
From the reflection my own.

SCORCH

here in my room alone i am going through my emotions like a fresh pack of cigarettes i break the plastic wrap and think of how you rapped my skull that night i think of how my body throbbed with pain as you lit me with joy as you hit me and put me between your lips our lust it burned my flesh that night and in delight i lay and waited, my breath baited like a fit for nicotine that night it seemed you'd crumble crush me to the end but now i wait for you again to take me here and mouth me to the snipe crush me to ashes scorch me till i'm out of sight

Lakey, the Sight

Of you tonight
Is a gaze at an eclipse,
Despair disguised by delight,
A kiss ending in a bite.

The truth which you have brought
Weighs down my tongue, clenches it,
Forces me to think of all the things
That don't need to be spoken. Let's skip

Paupers' graves of *How-We-Should* . Instead,
Taste my blood, swallow it in spoonfuls,
Smack the flavor, swish all my sentiments
Against gums. Paint your lips

With thoughts of me, feel how they ache.
When I embark and your arms are taut
From where I used to be, think
Of all the times we've shared;

Shackle memories of me around your wrists
Like amulets. Shake them, risk ridicule
The way I know you would, perform a ritual,
Shout. Draw your knees together fetal,

Shut your eyes, push away the outside world,
Disappear to a space our own. There, then
Listen to the metronome of your pulse
Throbbing quick with secret: it is I

Who skirts through the stream of your blood. Bear
Nothing else in memory, nothing else in mind;
If you will, shed tears on my behalf, shudder
And try to remember the gentle roar of my voice

As we continually live and die apart, together.

Those Final Moments

i sense an unfamiliar glisten in your eyes hiding beneath the dark locks of your hair tumbling forward as you stroke my cheekbones rub your fingers against flesh dust off my features whisper words of praise to me amidst flickers of candlelight swear that your love for me knows no constraints has no mercy is incapable of compromise and suddenly the absence of balance is obvious suddenly the tone of your voice is awry has a destructive feel seems foreign and suddenly this space of yours these walls which establish your room seem too close like they're closing themselves around in on me and i feel my limbs tremble and i wish i could move run away scream or do something anything other than helplessly lie here hopelessly lie here hopelessly feel like a spectator feel like a witness to some unspeakable event only this is not an event i mean this is my life yet you're lapping it up devouring it before me slicing pieces away with the sharp edge of your voice and i'm terrified terrified but this fear is a rush for me this fear lightens enlightens me with the powers of my life and my death and my desires my desires 'cause desire's running wild within me escalating like the thick patterns of incense in this room here i can neither moan nor gasp as i sense my lack of control my defeat to your hunger the loss of my breath while my chest is collapsing my loins are burning i feel i'm about to explode and you tell me you love me you own me while your fingers cold as steel strong and hard as machinery tighten their grip on my neck and steadfastly tenaciously twist

ANYTHING

Because it was too hot to reason,
And I was too bored to care,
I followed him through the door
But didn't say much,

Didn't want to make up lies
To match his when he said
That he found me fascinating,
Had always wondered about me,

Always wondered what I was like.
That made me smile
As he stripped down before me,
Rubbed his hardness against me,

Asked if anything was wrong.
"Only everything," I reassured him,
Sure that he could never know
How stupid I felt dropping to my knees,
Telling myself
Anything will do
For someone tired and disgusted with life,

Thinking I should be grateful, glad
At least

At that moment

I had an anything

And he was mine

Latex Love Letter

cluttered apart-
ment, alone:

night eases itself on
like a dark satin stocking I

follow suit with my clothes
naked and spread out

like something some-
body'd spilled there, like

letters of an alphabet–ya–can't
decipher language coaxing

flip through these yellowed
pages of me; bathe me in latex

clothing tightly
over skin used

to being used

translate my shivers beneath
silicone to those of slickly

bound presented
magazines thick as the desire dang–

ling in this monologue I've
been revising in my head

for so long, wanting
to believe wrapped tight

in latex I'm
a letter: lick

me at the edges, stamp
me, send me out.

YEAH, SURE

Yeah, sure
it was explosive when we met each other;
I can still remember the way my body trembled
at the thought of your touch
and the way I
never seemed to notice
the way I was exhausted
from all the hours of sleep I missed
just so I could feel myself
snuggled in the warmth of your voice

Yeah, sure
it hurt when I thought you didn't love me
after all, I had always hoped
for some strange reason
things would work out like
some cheesy '50s sitcom for us
and I have to admit that

Yeah, sure
I was surprised when I heard you finally admit
that your dark eyes
wanted something from me with some meaning
(something lasting)
something we could somehow call our own
and

Yeah, sure
the timing may have been a bit off
when I held you but
I knew that I had to keep an eye on my bags
that were carefully packed
like some guarantee for a package-deal future
that now seemed just one step closer
(although I had to go one step farther away)
but I promise to
religiously write you;
I'll miss you / I love you
I always think about you

but things somehow move a bit fast
and

Yeah, sure
I guess the months have skittered by
but I've been suffocating in a pile of new work
and I just thought I'd call to apologize
for losing track of all the letters I owe
and phone calls I meant to return
and no, I wasn't kidding when I said
that you still mean the world to me
and I promise that I'll come to visit you soon

Yeah, sure.

A SHEDDING OF SKINS

PARTY FAVORS

One Saturday afternoon I woke up in Couch Hall and found Justine next to me in my dinky loft bed. She was nudging my shoulder and saying my name over and over and over in a tone so annoying it managed to snatch me out of speed psychosis and deep sleep. I'd been crashed out and completely incoherent for a couple of days, as I'd started the week with a crystal meth study session that sped me through ninety-two hours of note cards and midterm exams, then dumped me on my ass. Breaking my slumber was no minor task.

"Wha? Huh? Nnnng." My voice sounded gravelly and thick, like chat sprinkled over mucous.

"Whew! Wake up and smell the addict," Justine said with a friendly grimace and turned her head. I was embarrassed at the thought that my breath could've melted plastic, but my attention was diverted by what I discovered on her neck: two oval-shaped whelps. Bruises.

Head propped on my pillow, I focused, looked at the bluish-purple stains on her ivory skin. The right one was about an inch higher than the one on its left. I passed my index finger over them, pressed, then examined my flesh. No traces of the pattern had rubbed off. I studied the smudges again. They stared back at me like an ominous second pair of eyes.

"Pretty gruesome, huh? I already checked 'em out in the mirror." Justine talked to the air, didn't look in my direction. "Great craftsmanship, Clint. Too bad I don't own a turtleneck dress."

I hated when she spoke away from me like that, as if a movie camera were hidden somewhere and she gave the audience an aside, secret information. It dawned on me the deal was that those spots on her neck were hickeys, ugly marks I must have left, but I was too groggy and apathetic to analyze if I was supposed to derive some deep meaning from her body language. Besides, I knew Justine would handle it for me.

"Okay, Master of the Obvious. What do I need to do, crush your skull for a wake-up call? Try this: *Tonight*. Can we say *Busted* ?" Justine asked, her mouth widening around the words with ironic ease.

She tilted her bleach-blonde head, locked her green eyes on mine, and everything seemed to be in slow motion. My muscles went loose and fluid. An icy wave of understanding crashed and hit me: *Fall Fling*.

"Fuck," I groaned, an image of the big picture filling my mind: Justine, David, Lakey, the shellacked social bit. I closed my eyes, wanted nothing more than to sleep and to skip the whole scenario. Justine pulled back my covers, yanked me wide awake instead.

"Uh-uh. Don't even *think* you can back out now, asshole! We've already gone through with the hassle of getting props, and it won't be long till the credits start rolling."

Our props. The big production. She made that night sound like some gala event.

Fall Fling was a formal dance at Hendrix that happened every year, just like all the other aged and crumbly pieces of Americana served at lots of colleges lots of places I've made fun of lots of times. And yet I'd reduced myself to another microwave pizza box lining of a student among the masses so desperate for entertainment that they'll eagerly shuck out 200-plus bucks for a rented outfit, buffeted dinner, and badly-d.j.ed dance. I didn't even have an ulterior motive, a plan to sabotage it: no maraschino cherries glued to my private parts, no liquid acid to spike the punch. In fact, none of us did.

For various reasons, we'd decided to go and play our parts, as if they actually were important. My motive was because I hadn't gone to prom in high school – well, I'd gone to prom but was too much of an outcast to actually make it inside; I dropped acid in the school parking lot, then snuck into a sleazy dance club instead – I thought Fall Fling might fill the gargantuan hole in my collegiate life where something was obviously missing. You know, give me stability, fill a void, make me normal. Group therapy type stuff. That and simply the age and the stage, a time in my life when everything seemed so monumental, especially downplaying its importance.

So anyway, I remember talking about it with David one afternoon while we got baked between classes.

"Man, just think how terrible it'll be!" he said, a glazed smile on his face as he passed the joint to me. "Everybody'll be runnin' around with poofy dresses in pastel colors and frosty pink lipgloss, bein' all royalty about it over nothin' more than a few extra streamers in that same ol' ballroom."

David, Justine, and I often ridiculed the event when we were polluted, went on and on about how it'd suck with sharp fangs. We even joked that we should save all the receipts of expenses related to it and make a contest out of whom had wasted the most money. Then again, "wasted" was quite a word in demand that first trimester of my sophomore year, a term when I stayed so high that brain cells and ideas came and went as rapidly as skywriting.

My designated date for the evening was Lakey, a friend of mine I'd gone out with once or twice. We met during orientation week of the new year, and I surreptitiously crowned her my official 'Romantic Conquest of the Season.' With her big blue eyes, heart-shaped face, and cropped golden hair, she was one of the few fresh faces on campus that seemed interesting, even remotely intense. Besides, I figured she'd help perpetuate the myth that I was bisexual — one of those fence-straddling lies concocted by timid gays and a somewhat trendy excuse for why I didn't have a steady boyfriend — as if I just couldn't be bothered, simply couldn't be tied down.

Lakey and I would have passionate conversations about our dreams, our aspirations in life. Nonetheless, I scrapped my interest in her as a paramour not long after I'd committed to the dance. Not only did she not find the notion of Fall Fling humorous, but she also confessed that she couldn't be my girlfriend unless I "converted" from my sinful life as a bisexual because her parents were missionaries and they'd never accept me. The romance/bleeding hearts and roses bit ended then. I couldn't believe she'd tried the Southern Baptist rebirth bit on me, but that didn't mean we couldn't hang out. She continued to sit beside me everyday in Fine Arts class, sent me cryptic letters through campus mail, and for some unfathomable reason still believed I'd be a suitable escort for a school dance.

We'd planned the event as a double date with Justine and David. Although Lakey didn't know them very well, it was a fairly basic formula: Lakey would go with me; Justine would go with David; the four of us would go together.

Easy enough, except for the variables that'd been added to the equation by the time our 'big day' rolled around. Unlike Lakey and me, Justine and David were officially a couple who'd established the illusion they were monogamous and in love. I suppose that's what they thought they should do: be something, stand for something. I'd known them since my freshman year and might have fallen for it — or at least considered that they believed in it themselves — if they hadn't been messing around with me on the side. Since this was at the stage before we were bold or chemically altered enough for threesomes, my escapades with each of them were random and quite secretive.

Justine and David had been an item for approximately a month when Justine brought me into the picture with her casual "Sure, I care about David, but that doesn't mean I couldn't care about you, too." Less than a week later, David made advances of his own, groping at me and gasping that he was "cool with the idea of experimentation" but he "wanted to keep stuff a secret because he didn't want to hurt Justine's feelings or cause her to break up." Yeah, sure.

As far as it went with me, they were sexy and mean-spirited, so their excuses didn't mean much. I assumed they were restless and bored with the whole commitment thing and thought an affair would bring new excitement, or at least function as a commercial break. You know, sort of up the ante. Whatever the case, the less they revealed about their interests in me, the more it completely turned me on. Justine was a costume designer, David was a painter, and I was single: the way I figured it, we were already well-versed enough in solitude, soul-searching, and suffering through our do–it–for–art type of ways that we could've talked a lifetime of possibilities. All I wanted to do was fuck. Fuck and be friends, of course.

The problem — as if there were just one — was the only person I really wanted to sleep with was David. Okay, not necessarily only, but primarily. Sex with Justine was more like some passive-aggressive act of vengeance. I mean, sure I was attracted to her and all, but more in the sense of wanting to be her than be with her. However, it was no secret to me what David's interest in her was: I watched the way he became transfixed on her, the way Justine made him sloppy and drooly and awkward like a drunk who can't stand up on his own. Unlike me, David was one of those hopelessly heterosexual boys who wiggled their toes in queer waters in an attempt to be a little less dry straight-white-male and a little more cool and cosmopolitan. Very '90s. Very MTV late-night. Very very. Since I'd been infatuated and disastrously suicidal over a few of those bisexual-chic boys back in high school, I'd come to recognize the type. I couldn't help the way they made me tingle in the groin, but I figured I could at least prevent myself from falling in love. I didn't want to fall in anything. I wanted to take prisoners.

I was Mr. Mistress to both parties in a "don't ask, don't tell" guise of a relationship. Admittedly, it might not sound like much, but there once existed a page in time when this tabloid-worthy title functioned as an ego-inflator and source of entertainment. Meals in the cafeteria were no longer flat and unappealing; they turned spicy and stimulating when Justine played games of footsie under the table and David surreptitiously caressed my knees and inner thighs — particularly if both my friends flirted at the same time. I loved watching them simultaneously attempt to hide their motives; it was like having my own private film. But nothing compared to the thrills I got from familiar knocks or frenzied raps at my dorm door during sex when I knew it was my, our, other lover who stood outside. Within the span of a few seconds, I'd freeze up, fuck like a possessed fiend, and then scream orgasmic resurrections into my pillow. The whole scenario was almost too hot for me to keep secret. If I weren't already in awe at how nobody − not even my terminally curious roommate, Michael − appeared to notice what was going on, I'm sure I wouldn't have.

"Think I should wear a choker or something? There's no way I'm gonna try the old trick with the scarf." Justine positioned herself before the mirror on my wall, considered different poses as I dressed.

"Just motor it, okay? We've gotta do some killer brainstorming to pull this one off," she said. I smiled and led the way out my door, tried to put a plan in motion I'd yet to devise myself.

We searched around campus, asked advice from people we thought we could trust. Around four o'clock, we found our chum Mandy, who loaned us makeup that must've been intended for mummies. It was thick as plaster and looked just as fake, air bubbles clustered around the lid of the container like tiny insects trapped in amber, the bottom portion of the glass jar noticeably thicker and whiter where makeup had settled. I studied the color separation, a spectrum of graceful folds that reminded me of diagrams I'd seen of soil layers, and wondered if we could match any of the shades to Justine's skin.

"I know how it is, man. But this stuff is the shit," Mandy assured, took the container from my hands and tapped the aluminum lid with her scrawny forefinger. "A friend of mine turned me on to it when my complexion was really gnarly, and it worked wonders. It's made for burn victims so they can, like, cover up their scars, you know? Heavy duty. Just keep slapping on layers till the color's right."

"I'm sold," Justine said. "Seems like the ammo we need to fight that whole confessional bit, huh, Clint?"

"Totally," Mandy answered, her female voice in place of mine.

"I mean anything, absolutely anything to prevent some heartfelt moment tonight. We can go into the melodrama after I feature my new black velvet dress."

Mandy laughed her orangutan laugh and nodded her head in agreement, her reddish-orange corkscrew curls bouncing like miniature Slinkies.

"How could the night go bad, as long as I look good?" Justine asked, rhetorically. Words of wisdom from the girl whose motto was 'appearance is everything.'

"Are you for real?" I muttered.

"I'm real popular," Justine punctuated with a jab of her chin.

I took a deep breath. We'd scored, so we left Mandy's room and headed towards our dorm.

Justine seemed full of herself and the plan to fool David. She was oblivious to my silence as we walked across the parking lot, each step I took on the pavement a harsh reminder of other subplots, private productions I thought I should put on myself. I drifted in and out as she rambled about how she'd had a hellacious hickey experience back in high school but the whole thing was funny now so she guessed it wouldn't have been a big deal if we wouldn't have gotten the makeup because she and David weren't gonna last forever anyway because nothing really lasts, you know? But then of course everybody knows that, even if they pretend they don't, but actually she guessed it sucked more to know there's no point in anything because once people realize everything is pointless, what's the point in even making a point about how pointless it is?

Which is exactly how I found Justine's *Cliffs' Notes* attempt at philosophy: ironically insipid and trite. It was the black blaze on the opposite end of the parking lot that startled me. David. He was early, had returned from his out-of-town excursion a couple hours sooner than we anticipated. I felt the pavement begin to turn to quicksand beneath my feet.

"Shit!" Justine hissed and ran towards the dorm, slid through its doors in a blur before I could respond.

After all the times Justine witnessed me weasel my way out of trouble with police officers or parents, I assume she entrusted me to have some smooth-sounding one-step solution. I didn't. David was one of the few people who stifled my ability to ad-lib.

I had no idea what to say or how to act, so I tried to at least smile as I stood there and watched him approach me. It's weird what goes on when you're attracted to someone. My heart pounded louder and louder the closer he got, a strange sort of Doppler effect.

"She just started her period," I lied before he had a chance to ask. "It weirds her out. You know, cramps and massive mood swings. Way Richter. Head over to my room with me, though, and help me pick out what I should wear tonight."

His face seemed to stretch with surprise, eyebrows raised the same shape children draw as a bird in flight. "You haven't decided yet?"

"Uh, no," I said and hooked my arm through his, which was usually as affectionate as we'd get in public. "I mean, I have a rental jacket, but I need a second opinion. You know how it goes."

How it goes is where we went: my cluttered dorm room. Check this out for decor.... There were two large windows that I'd covered with shiny black plastic garbage bags and blocked with my loft bed, so the only light in the room was one of those glaring 1000-watt jobs, which I'd dimmed with a black tulle drape. Charcoal black carpet covered the floor, and grainy black–and–white photocopied pictures of hairsprayed-nightmare death rock bands and pseudo-erotic images (of latex-clad models, a naked man with an erupting champagne bottle covering his crotch, ad nauseam) covered everything else. They were Scotch-taped everywhere, literally – on the garbage bags, the ceiling, the backside of the door. I'd worked diligently to transform the 12' x 12' lair into an installation art piece, a tribute to twenty-nothing angst, complete with matching wardrobe.

"Look what I brought," David said as he produced two bottles of Riunite Royal Raspberry from his backpack. "Party favors." He smiled, obviously proud of himself, screwed the cap off one of the bottles and took a slug.

Lakey phoned from her room on the third floor. "Are you guys ready?"

"Are you serious?" I was incredulous. It was barely after 5 p.m. "What's the big rush? I mean, why is everybody so early?"

"Boring, bored, boredom." She sighed into the receiver. "Besides, my roommate needs the room so she and her boyfriend can, um, you know."

"Bump uglies?" I suggested.

"So eloquent."

"Thanks. Listen," I told her, "I'm still getting dressed, but feel free to come down. Maybe David and I can entertain you, Miss Bor—"

"Deal," she said, the rest drowned out by a click and hum of the receiver. Lakey arrived within seconds.

"Where's your roomie?" she asked as she let herself in.

"Oh, you know: out of town, out of mind."

I felt out of my mind — bummed, burnt-out, bananas. My entire body was suffering from sensory overload – shock frustration fear excitement lust disgust – too much at once, too much for it to handle. It had run out of juice and I didn't blame it. In dire need of assistance, I excused myself and headed to the bathroom to snort some of the 'emergency reserve' of speed I had stashed in my pants pocket. Unfortunately, I'd already consumed the good stuff and had to resort to crank.

I entered the last stall numbly, tore open the corner of a ziploc, a makeshift baggie, and dumped the contents on top of the toilet paper dispenser. The drugs were filthy: not just cut but plague-brown and chunky, the consistency of peanut butter. And the smell. The smell was overwhelming, chemical and deadly and singeing my nostril hairs. *Some biker probably whipped up this batch with battery acid* , I thought, chopping the mounds into lines with my student i.d. Then of course I hoovered it, chain-snorted all four rails.

I whisked out of the stall and stood in front of the bathroom mirror, stared at myself a few seconds and watched my pupils grow larger, eclipse the blue of my eyes. I spoke to my reflection, pep-talked the situation:

"Okay, you're going to be fine. You can handle this." I shuddered from the drip, toxins fizzling down the back of my throat. "Do a blast; have a blast" was my mantra.

My eyes teared up and my stomach gave a sick rumble. I dashed back into the stall and dropped my trousers in panic, barely managing to make it. My intestines exploded with a wet yelp. I had a scorching case of diarrhea.

I extricated myself after that unfortunate experience and veered back to my room, limbs overly-anxious and jittery, jaw clenched.

"Hey," I said as I closed the door behind me. My voice was dry, foreign. Fearing my features were in manic contortions, I fought to keep my upper lip from twitching.

Lakey was sipping wine, swaying her hips to the Orb CD they'd put in my player. Completely oblivious. But David took one look at me and asked, "What were you doing? Mining the ol' nose gold?"

Then, before I could answer, he sneered, "I hate when you do that shit."

I hate when it makes me shit, I thought, dabbing traces of sweat off my forehead with the sleeve of my tuxedo. *I hate when it makes me feel like shit.*

Three agonizing hours, countless restroom excursions and enough small talk and shirt changes to chap my skin later, Justine came downstairs to my room. She looked beautiful: snow blonde hair pulled back except for an elegant curl on each temple, smoky makeup carefully smudged around emerald eyes, lips shiny and red, flawless cover-up on her neck, and a slinky size seven dress. It was almost enough to make me forget babysitting David and dealing with his mixed body language and Lakey's annoying "Can we go yet?"

I don't think anybody asked Justine about her delay. We were all ecstatic to leave my room; there are few things worse than being dressed up to get messed up but feeling bored and restless.

Dinner was the first stop on our agenda, so we squeezed into David's black Mazda. It was rickety and far from well-kept, but since we wanted to go to Little Rock and David was the only one among us who owned an automobile, our options were limited.

His car made rattling noises as soon as we started moving, which distracted from our intentions of creating a glamorous veneer, even if we were impeccably dressed. Lakey wore a red sequined gown, and my game of magical shirts concluded with a frilly white Renaissance replica. Eyeliner fag stuff. Regardless, before we'd even crossed Conway's city limits, tension had begun to descend on us like patches of the ceiling's cloth that drooped and brushed against our heads.

Thirty miles of pavement later, we reached Little Rock and its five-building skyline. David swerved and took the downtown exit. Through the course of the drive, we'd learned that Lakey didn't want to eat Chinese food or oysters because they were too far "out there"; David couldn't eat most dairy products due to his allergies; Justine wouldn't eat in a restaurant with meat aromas because she'd been a vegetarian most of her life and the smell of "rotting flesh" would make her hurl; I preferred to avoid garlic and onions because I didn't want to be stuck with coyote breath, and none of us had tried sushi. Yet where and what we *would* eat was still a mystery.

We drove up and down Kavanaugh, Cantrell, Rodney Parham, reading illuminated signs and tossing their names back and forth like some kind of twisted tennis match. It all seemed too complex. Where we ate didn't matter much to me – my stomach was knotted with nervousness and third-rate amphetamines, so I didn't have much of an appetite – but it seemed to be a crucial concern to everyone else, especially Lakey. She lost it when David made a joke that we could always go to Burger King and "have it our way."

"Is that supposed to be funny? Well, ha ha ha. Now get me out of this tin can of a car before I fuckin' lose my mind!"

I saw David's glare in the rearview mirror. Justine shot me a wide-eyed look from the passenger seat, a silent scream of *I understand*. I couldn't help but laugh my fake lithium laughter. I'd assumed the production of Fall Fling would be ridiculous, but we were acting much worse ourselves.

David pulled into the parking lot of The Villa, an Italian restaurant, before Lakey had a chance to bust out a window or lash out at anyone else.

We entered the foyer and were greeted by aromas of pasta, buttered bread, and a poofy-haired hostess who informed us there'd be approximately a half-hour wait. Lakey let out a long sigh of impatience.

"Aw, let's just stick it out and have a few drinks. We won't even notice the time," I said and threaded my fingers through hers for added emphasis. I knew it was around ten o'clock, the time Fall Fling was scheduled to start back at Hendrix, but I'd already tired of the dinner/dance ritual and just wanted to be done with it.

They agreed, but less than five minutes passed until we changed our minds. The bartender refused to serve Lakey because she didn't have proof of age. Since that was something none of us could legally prove, it became imperative to find another restaurant. I was painfully aware of the different moods we were in, understood the body language too well, and needed liquor to calm my nerves, to change that. Fast. Booze has never been a big deal to me, but since I was supposed to be Lakey's date, I figured it would be the least confrontational choice of substance abuse. I would've snorted or smoked or shot just about anything to replace reality with a grin on my face, to induce a pseudo state of happiness.

David drove to an industrial area at the edge of town and parked at a building with a green neon Spaghetti Warehouse sign. Italian seemed to be a safe choice. We entered the restaurant as sophisticated, semi-intelligent people, and were seated almost instantly.

Our waiter's name was Eduardo, or at least that's what his name-tag said. He was short and skinny and swish-hipped, and looked about as Italian as his frosted hair looked natural.

"Could I get you all some drinks?" he asked with a wink. "Screwdriver? Bloody Mary? Vodka Cranberry?"

His enthusiasm to prove his hipness was nauseating. I'm sure he didn't think any of us were legal, but he took the "big buddy in crime" approach because he wanted a hefty tip.

Whatever his motives, we were all pleased he brought us a bottle of red wine.

We sat and sipped, uneasily trying to stir up conversations by telling outlandish stories of our pasts, tales of old friends nobody else knew. Nonetheless, they turned hopelessly lame within minutes, and a silence hit us with the impact of asphalt. I felt my mind stretching, frantically trying to come up with something to talk about. Appearance may be everything, but it's a pretty dull show without dialogue or a soundtrack.

Eduardo brought another bottle of wine at David's request.

A hand squeezed my knee. I had no idea who was responsible, so I tried to casually glance around the room. Consequently, I discovered we were the only people left in the restaurant. It was late: 20 past 11, according to my watch.

"Hey, do you think we should make our way to the dance soon? It'll be midnight by the time we make it there." My voice didn't sound like my own.

"Sure," Justine said and slowly nodded. She didn't seem miffed by anything. "So I guess that means we're not gonna get anything to eat then?"

"Oh yeah, *food*," Lakey said with a slow, thick laugh. I could tell she was drunk because she didn't have anything else to say on the subject, not even after her tantrum.

Justine rolled her eyes and sighed. "Yeah, food. Very good. Are we getting it, or what?" she asked, coldhearted and bored. At that moment, I loved her, loved her emptiness. It seemed so much easier than being analytical and deep. Battling my mix of emotions was exhausting; I wanted nothing more than to feel less.

As if by cue, Eduardo appeared at our table. David ordered spaghetti with red sauce, the most boring dish imaginable; I ordered tortellini alfredo, my favorite; Lakey requested a plate so she could "have a few bites of mine" and ordered a piece of chocolate cake; Justine ordered a Stoli and soda with lemon.

"That's all you want?" David asked and smoothed his hand across her shoulder.

Justine cringed at his touch, forced what almost was a smile.

"Sure, I guess." She batted her mascaraed eyelashes. "But first I need to go fix my lipstick. Excuse me."

She pushed herself from the table, and Lakey followed. David watched them disappear through the bathroom door; then he turned to me.

"Clint, *Clint*," he whispered and leaned forward, quickly pressed his lips against mine. "Be honest with me. Is something going on?"

"Going on?" I took a big gulp of my wine, tried to act innocent.

"Yeah, *going on*. Did you tell Justine about us or something? She's acting really weird."

"Weird? Um, no. She doesn't know about us," I said, a weak attempt to dismiss the whole thing. "I didn't tell her anything."

"Does she- Is she- Hiding something from me? Involved with somebody else?

An entire world laid between that instant and the evening we'd been planning. I looked at David. His face was slender and French-looking, his nose without a bridge. Veins faintly glowed a reddish-purple through his pale and shallow skin. I looked away.

"Is something up between you and her?"

There was the humming of fluorescent lights. My heart beat like a sped-up metronome, pounding on its maximum setting. My bowels – well, forget about my bowels. I tried to avoid David, but I couldn't help myself. In an impulse of compassion or guilt or vindictiveness, I told him the truth.

He looked at me a moment with wide eyes, cheeks pink with embarrassment or rage; then he looked down. I knew he had known it all along.

"Could we just wait and talk about it after tonight? Please? Just till after the dance?" I asked, almost pleading.

We have to make it to the formal, I thought. *At least make an appearance. Show. If we make it to Fall Fling, everything'll be just fine.*

A line from a short story called "Fleeting Happiness" came to mind, in which Cookie Mueller declares that "Happiness if a fictitious feeling... To know the truth — life is hard, and then you die — isn't a very comfortable thing to live with. If everyone knew the cold facts, the sky would be darkened with falling bodies in suicide leaps."

I had pawned our final fleeting moment of happiness for the truth, but I wasn't really prepared to deal with the result in a stoic manner. On the contrary, the red wine had started to give me a buzz and violent throb of passion, or passionate confusion. Or whatever.

Fall Fling and good Zing, that is. Some killer crystal would clear my mind. Make me get in control.

Justine and Lakey returned from the john. David sat silently, his head propped on his hand, sharp chin digging into his palm.

Didn't I stash a spare baggie somewhere last week? Inside a CD case? Beneath my jewelry box?

"We're back," Justine said as she seated herself. She gave me a quick grin and slipped her lips to the wine glass.

"He told me, Justine." David's voice was deadpan, calm.

My stomach growled in defiance.

"Told you?" Justine giggled. I watched her grip on the stem of her glass tighten, her knuckles turn white.

"Look, I *know*, Justine. About you two. He told me."

"Wha...?" Lakey's mouth dropped open in confusion, in disbelief.

"You told him what?" Justine asked, her eyes glaring at mine, her tone pure exasperation.

"You... are... terrible," David muttered.

"Oh, and I suppose you're a hell of a lot better?"

During the course of the last few weeks, everything in my life had accelerated: sex with David in his car or at his brother's place in Little Rock, sex with Justine on whims in study rooms around campus, small-talk with Lakey, my pile of incomplete assignments, my drug intake. I'd lived for the day and stretched myself out like elastic until the day when this inevitable confrontation popped up and slapped me across the face.

"What the hell!" Lakey blurted, her voice sounding too big for her.

"I should've known better than to mess with you bisexuals." She said bisexuals in italics. "Disgusting – immoral... flakes! You can't make up your minds about anything."

One thing was for sure: Lakey was right about that one.

While her comment hung in the air, I made a decision. I began taking mental snapshots of the people in front of me, capturing details of the party favors I'd mistaken as friends: Lakey's bee-stung lips a luscious red that matched her cheeks and gown, Justine's cool posing that cracked open with confusion, David's wet eyes and clenched fists. They seemed as anonymous and transparent as characters I could have created, characters in a story that so desperately needed a rewrite. Anonymous because they were people, yet I'd been treating them as objects, things.

Eduardo brought our entrees, but I can't recall if anyone ate. We split the check four ways, gathered up ourselves and left, headed back to Hendrix.

Outside it was raining, lightly sprinkling, more like gauze than a splatter.

David shuffled around between the seats, then fed a Lush cassette into his player and started the ignition. Nobody spoke. The only words that passed between us were the singer's muted lyrics, distorted by his car's speakers. My thoughts sort of frittered around. I slouched down in my seat behind Justine, the back of her skull a whitish orb resting above the passenger headrest, glowing in the depthless black field of my peripheral vision.

"Should you be driving?" Lakey asked.

"Sure," David nodded, clicked on the windshield wipers. *Whoosh, whoosh.* "I'm fine. Fine," he said, glaring at Justine instead of the rearview mirror as he backed into a parked car. *Bam!*

"Shit!" I gazed into the shadows behind us and the words escaped me: "Drive! I think there's somebody in there!"

Then I faced forward, afraid I might become a pillar of salt. "I *said,* fucking DRIVE, David!"

And with that, he crammed the car into gear, and we squealed out of the parking lot.

Traffic was a blur of streaming light.

"Are they behind us? Is anyone behind us?" David asked, hunched forward on the steering wheel, his knuckles white.

"No," I said, looking over my shoulder again. "The coast is—"

"DAVID!" Justine interrupted. "WE'RE ON THE WRONG SIDE OF THE ROAD!"

It took a few seconds for the information to register, but we were. We were traveling south on the northbound interstate, a concrete median separating us from the side of the highway where we should have been.

"Ohh..." David groaned, "Whoa! What— What do I do?"

"What do you do?" Justine asked incredulously. "What do you do!" That one was punctuated by a pickup truck whizzing by, its horn blaring.

"Turn the car around," I urged.

"Around? Just turn it around?"

"Yes, *around,* idiot," Justine hissed through her teeth.

A moment's breath, then David flipped a bitch, squealing tires and barely missing a vehicle as we pivoted in the right direction. He managed to thwack Justine's head against the side window in the process, which added humor to the situation (though her squeal didn't sound like she found it very funny). I bit my cheeks to strangle a laugh.

My bowels had loosened in the shock of our collision antics and were urgently demanding to be voided, but short of further prolonging the histrionics by asking David to find a public restroom, there was nothing to be done but clench my muscles and wait it out.

"I'm going home," David announced as we entered the dorm parking lot, his voice brittle. He didn't look at us as Lakey, Justine and I piled out of the car. In fact, he didn't even get out to inspect his vehicle. No one did but me; it looked fine as he sped away.

Lakey walked briskly, whisked through the dorm's glass doors. Justine and I sauntered silently, a slow and unremarkable yet major task at the moment, the cold night air oppressive. I don't remember what I said to her, if anything. What I do remember is feeling dizzy. Dizzy and drained. And what I remember most is thinking that I should be thinking or feeling something, something else.

Justine went to her room or wherever and I went to the bathroom. Again. And again.

So we never even made it to Fall Fling. Barely one a.m. and alone in my room, eyes clinging to my digital alarm clock as it ticked away the evening, I wondered how I could or if I should apologize. Somehow I doubted Hallmark would have a condolences card for such a fiasco.

As I dusted off the leftover bottles of Riunite and passed out in my tux, it hit me that all the nothing that comprised my everything was bullshit. None of us was saved in time, before the credits rolled. And I really had no clue who or what it was I wanted, but I couldn't wait to get there.

In the weeks to come, I played the revised, corrected version of this night in a torturous tape loop. I'd never intended to make such a mess of things. Really, I hadn't. I merely thought my past needed a little "fixer-upping"; as if upgrading my party favors – i.e. making things look "right" or "better" – would transform my life into an exciting, newsworthy whirl of happiness and excessive pleasure. Natch, the things I needed to fix weren't dates or dances. But that would come later. Much later. First I had to ditch the bisexual bit; then I had to conclude that I didn't want to take prisoners; I wanted to fall in love, although of course I had to learn to love myself and all that blah blah yakkety I won't go into here. If I did, this story would turn into a 12-step self-help anecdote instead of the tragicomedy it really is.

Anyway, Fall bled into Winter bloomed into Spring, and my friendships with David, Justine and Lakey gradually vanished into the ozone, which should come as no surprise. We went through various cycles of resentment and reprieve; we went through numerous hairstyles and colors. We even swapped up our pairings and went to Spring Fling (Lakey escorted by David, Justine by me). Almost immediately upon our arrival, I became unnervingly aware of the vast, unbreachable distance between the cinematic dream of my imagination (that the dance would make everything "all right") and the lame, undoubtedly real school function I couldn't wait to leave. That's when I concluded there wasn't any ritual that'd fill the hole in my life. And the powder I continued shovelling up my nostrils didn't fill the void, it just increased it.

Incidentally, these realizations were by no means solutions. I still had many moons and miles to go of trying the same chemical insanity in different settings and expecting different results. Needless to say, I had great difficulty coming to terms with the fact that the glory days were over. Until I could reinvent myself and my fixes of choice – the things that set me off, keep me going – I continued stumbling glossy-eyed through nightmares of my own creation, waiting to be filled with hope that maybe tomorrow would be the day I'd wake up and my real life would start.

First Person Third Person First

Unfolded: that free
Verse of a boy who

Five-fingered the story his
Life has become. Un-

Folded: first from feet
To head, when he heard of, met

Syllabic feet, learned to walk with
Stress, unstress, stride from line

To line, keep step
With iamb, with

Trochee. The subtleties
Of language he

Learned through red and
Pink of flesh of

Body, the con-
text his body-of-the became

A place in which to play, dabbling
In the figurative and

The descriptive, flirting
Around with tropes, developing

His diction along with the new
Possibilities of / for his

Skin. The movement
Of the body is

Where poetry
Begins

GUESS i shouLd ṭAlk AbOuṭ SEX

It's a common point of interest
People are either having it or
They've had it or
They'll pretend they have if they haven't
What else would they say
With the American way of
Live and get laid
No matter what class or
Color or creed,
The notion of sex weaves and
Wiggles its way like earthworms
Through the layers of thoughtsoil
In our brains

Sex is one of the first words that
We hear and first words
We retain: what child could ignore
An arrangement of letters small enough
To be whispered but large enough
To stick out of conversations as if
It were the limb of a tree
Sturdy, bulky, branching from
Face to name to city to state to
Everywhere everyhow everything
Sex is linked
It brought all of us into existence
And has proven it's here to stay

So I guess I should talk about it
Though I haven't had much luck
In the past
I tossed the term around
In my little-boy sentences
At age eight or nine but
Figured out somebody must have forgotten
To include instructions for its use
I knew I'd done something wrong
When I sent my grandma into a

Red-faced wheezing fit from
Which she barely recovered and
Wheezed my mom away much
The same: she stiffened and
Was replaced by a scientist who
Spoke in a sterile language composed
Of polysyllabic terms
She held me in her lap
And pointed to colored diagrams
That were supposed to explain
The concept of intercourse to me
I thought they were puzzles
But my dad was puzzling, too
When I showed him a pin-up shot
From *Hustler* magazine that
I'd found in our ditch, he gave
A nervous laugh and grumbled
That I'd understand someday
I wanted to understand *then*
My curiosity was a short fuse burning furiously
Just like most other people's though
They rarely want to admit it so
I guess I should talk about sex
I thought it was the center of the universe
When I was in high school, anyway
I was a horny little fucker
Whose cock jumped to attention
At the thought of getting play
I was so full of testosterone
I'm surprised I didn't leave a trail behind me
But at least fucking wasn't
The only thing on my mind
I didn't see the point in raving about it
'cause years of locker room chat among pimply boys
Had tread that territory well into the ground
I may have just been sixteen but
I was sick to death of stories from peons
Like Marty Pope, the inbred brain-dead
Bendable straw of a boy who never ceased
To boast about bitches who loved to suck his dick
We all knew he was lying which

Was pointless and pathetic
I wanted to talk about sex that wasn't fairytale
I wanted to talk about sex that's raw and
Real and ugly at times
I wanted to talk about sex in a world
With disease and rape and abuse
But nobody wanted to talk about it with me
And they especially didn't want to listen
Didn't want to relate it to themselves
So I decided to do an independent study
For my Gifted-and-Talented class (what a gas)
I interviewed a friend whose innocence
Had been stained by the older boy next door
Who taught him how to play a game
He called 'motherfucker'
I stuck the interview among the stack
Of page after page of dehumanized statistics
I had collected for my paper
I wanted to talk about sex
And I didn't want there to be distance
I wanted a primary source, an actual person
I wanted to let people know
That children are sexually abused
And it isn't just a problem off in a Bronx ghetto
Or a cop show on t.v.
Sexual abuse isn't a myth
And I was determined to slap the facts
Right in their faces, show
It ain't no Santa Claus so
It's time to stop smiling and
Covering up the topic and
Shoving it down the chimney
Enough shoving's already being done
Even right there, smack-dab in the middle
Of sickeningly Southern Jonesboro, Arkansas
And I knew because the anonymous friend
I had interviewed was
Actually me
Not that I had to worry about being discovered
Or anything, nobody paid attention when
I presented my project to the class

The students made fag jokes and snickered
And my teacher dismissed the interview
As if it weren't real
And I often wish myself it weren't
Which is exactly how I feel about
My four years of hell in high school
But I deal with the same archetypal assholes
Every day, I guess they
Never go away
They just go on blindly following
Ideals of right and wrong
Pseudo-morality has been fed to them
By the bucketful
And they've gobbled it up until
Life has become a big Puritanical euphemism
But that's not the way I want to go
No picture-perfect bullshit for me
I want a life that's REAL
A life with adjectives as jaded as I want them to be

So I guess I should talk about sex
And I'll talk about it without cracking dumb jokes
Or throwing in the routine "dude" and "man" garbage
Because I want people to think I'm straight
And I'll talk about it without being emasculated
By terms like orgasm and masturbation
And I'll talk about it to empower the role of
Rational, thinking humans instead of
Ignorant animalistic fuckmachines
And I'll talk about it
And I'll talk about it and
I'll scream if that's what it takes
To make people pay attention to topics that
Aren't lighthearted prime-time t.v. material,
Topics that might be kinky or race-related or
Gender-challenging or queer and
Even though there are a lot of other
Important issues in the world
I refuse to let another day pass in which
I demean or shadow the things
Directly related to me

'cause there's nobody else who'll do it
And a shitload of schmos who'd
Love to prevent it, I
Guess I should
Talk about sex.

EVERYBODY'S BIG EXCEPTION

I was branded 'Everybody's Big Exception'
Back in college, a nickname that came about
Because of the type of guys I shagged,
A pattern of boys that never messed around with boys
And swore they never, never would
Except that they did with me

Case in point: Capital D, a drawn-out disappointment
Among my collection of Nameless Faceless
Caucasian Straight-Male Closeted Cocksuckers
I wanted to believe he was different
When the thing we had began
He was hot and fun to hang out with
And a pretty decent fuck
Not that sex was the only thing between us
We were friends, so I expected more
Than the blow-and-go routine I'd had
With sluts or basic idiots

No power-play, I thought - no great demands
Or anything; we'd both agreed
Sex was no big deal so
We shouldn't make it that way
You know, it was all *casual* : we had
No need for the schmack about commitments or strings
We didn't even need to bring those topics up
Because we were so cool with everything
Except for when it worked my nerves
The times he'd start the bit about
How I was gay but he was straight
Just seconds short of when he'd grab my crotch
While mumbling shit about how sometimes
Other stuff just kinda happens
As he peeled off my pants
And *just kinda* did just that
When we were done
He'd go into his spiel of small talk
Before slipping in the nervous reminder that

Since we were so cool with everything
We didn't need to mention it to anybody else
They'd probably only screw things up, he said
How could they ever understand
A relationship like the one we had?

He'd stumble over his words
As he stumbled over his clothes
Reassuring that he didn't mean a
RELATIONSHIP relationship or anything,
But a relationship in the sense of
Like, a relationship with his brother,
You know? Only not really his brother
Because of course he couldn't get it on with him
But that wasn't to say he
Didn't love me like a brother
'cause, you know, I was such a special friend
And it was cool that we could hang out
Without me weirding over him or the fact
He's not into men or that whole homo scene
Everything was totally different with me
I'm nothing like the other guys he knows
In fact, he doesn't even think of me as male
I'm really rad, you know, an arty type
Which is why he could handle the
Occasional experimentation with me
He knew I really got into it
And he's cool enough that like, he didn't mind
A little sacrifice for his good buddy
Besides, what's an orgasm between friends, anyway?
And of course he wished he could hang out longer
But there was always some blah blah
Yakkety schmack excuse why he had to leave

As Everybody's Big Exception, I learned the routine fast
And thought that when we played the game
No one could win but me
When I had dirt on ones like D, guys that
Joe Castro Rainbow Flag a Go Go types
Worshipped like Adonis but
Shrugged off as "Lost Causes" or "Terminally Straight"

I'm ashamed to say I got a stupid sense of pride
From secrets that proved otherwise
I thought I had them by the balls
When they went off on all
Their tired attempts to lie and justify themselves

Each day of life as Everybody's Big Exception
Slapped the faces of Straight-power Shitheads
Who called me Death Rock Faggot
I thought I had prestige
As if some couture somebody-or-other
Deemed me the hot item
Heterosexual men should wear for the season
So I tried as many on for size
As I could and
For a while I felt good
Really fuckin' good
Till my delusional drugs wore off
As they should
Daylight came and I was forced to finally see
That what I thought were runways
Were only shady trails
To bushes or secluded parks
There's no love or romance to find
From backseat fucks in parking lots
And the inconvenience of hooking up
With D, or any other dumbass in denial,
Doesn't intensify the excitement
It's just an unwelcome pain in my ass
That leaves me with an empty bed in the morning
And a bowl of Told-You-So's for breakfast
It makes me sick to think of how long
I fed them to myself
As if life were nothing else than being stuck
Within the muck of Somewhere In Between
A constant state of insignificance
Emotionally fulfilling as a paperback romance
And frustrating as blue balls
Enough of that for me
I've had my fill of trivial garbage to know
The whole scene stinks

So for all you clueless codependent sods
Who think I'm a consolation prize
Or backup plan for lost girlfriends
Hear me out now:
I'm not the one
The language of cowardice
I neither understand nor speak
For love I'll sacrifice a lot
But my big exception
Is me.

i remember how i

Recklessly rode with you
On your 'cycle that night,
My stomach full of fear, bargain bin
Wine, and anticipation

I remember how I
Held you tight,
Slid my fingers onto the skin
Beneath your t-shirt,
Traced a trail to your heart via
Arms, shoulders, and tits
And felt a warmth
Which made me shudder.

There, on those two wheels
That night
We laughed, tasted the
Moist July air
As we yelled to each other
Of how the weeks had passed
So quickly and
How we had been, all
The things that had been
Going on

We paved the streets with disregard
And alcohol made me
Also disregard my mouth
We busted through the *No Trespassing* borders
Of hateful, homophobic Little Rock with
A vengeance the second that
All the things I'd never spoken
Leapt from my fingers, the instant
Each of my touches turned to grasp clutches
You shifted into autopilot, tried to

Casually drive, shout occasional small talk which
Maybe would've been fine but

Most of the time when you talked
While I touched you couldn't manage to do more
Than singe your coolness with fiery
Freudian slips. I thought they
Were cute, but the tension in your chest
Tipped me you felt otherwise

I thought about telling you we
Didn't have to limit ourselves to words but
That was around the same time that
You lowered my hand to your crotch
And the bulge there insisted you already knew, with
Cock revved-up and ready the
Things we could do, all the things for
Me and you, we were a testosterone tirade and
It felt like the world was ours for the taking,
So we did

And without trouble: there
Couldn't have been a small town street that
We overlooked we took 'em on
Full-forced we vandalized the Southern Baptist
Whitewash landscape, stained it with the sloppy paint
Of flaming faggot glares without
Any concern for asinine Arkansas, baby
You had a little rock of your own that
Reflected the rigidity of mine like
A rearview mirror so
I drove right into it
As we drove into the night, drove
Right into each other and
Our boysex came to life

There, on your 'cycle
Our blood rushed, pumped like gasoline
It was like we could've torched the whole
Fuckin' city with our combustion, man
Gushed out flames of fairie power by the gallons
Charred every last scrap of shrubbery,
Concrete, and chrome while
We skittered through the streets

Spat dust in the face of our past
Blinded the night with truthlight
Blessed the integrity of our bodies
Which hissed popped cracked
Exploded like ember grenades
Like multicolored comets of candor

I remember when we caused them
That night on your 'cycle
The night I claimed your flesh
As mine.

DANIELLE, I'VE BEEN MEANING TO TELL YOU

That of course I'd heard about you and
I always wondered if when we met
I'd piss my pants from the impact so
When that night finally came I guess
It should be expected that I was worried
You'd smell my fear like a rabid dog, but
You didn't, you didn't because
Fear for me wasn't there: I
Found you comforting rather than fierce
Which I probably shouldn't say
And actually I haven't because

Danielle, I've been meaning to tell you
Your words have followed me like frenzied stalkers
Since the first time I read them
On the subway, on side streets
They lurk behind me wherever I go they're
Even more vicious here in the city
Probably because they're at home but
No matter where it is I am
Your poems are my favorite bedtime stories
They take me to your graveyard of nightmares,
Lay me down, throw dirt in my face
I wouldn't care if you danced on my own because
My fingers and lips are stained from
Eating your verse by the mouthful yet
I'm not satisfied, always yearn for more
I'm hungry, but it's a hungry world

And I've been meaning to tell you
I can sense that it's beating you down
Which is nobody's surprise
Life has been a fucked-up song for
The both of us, and people always pelt
The singers out of tune as if
Human nature isn't bad enough,
We've got static to deal with, too
Smack fumes fogging your vision and

Sketch crackles surrounding me
Not that they really matter, anyway
You're like a broken mirror and
It scares me when my reflection's clear yet

Still I've been meaning to tell you
How weak I sometimes get when
You look at me with iced blue eyes,
Your skin alabaster powder, your
Hair fine shadow wisps but
I don't want you to think that
I have some stupid crush on you although
I'm not really sure myself so
You might be right if you did after
All, you wake my blood, speed it up
More than last night's quarter and
I'm always jonesing for more

And I've been meaning to tell you
I may be well-versed in small talk
But the night we were out
And you said that I'm perfect
I really didn't know how to respond I
Wondered if it was just the drugs talking
Besides, you're a plague filled with pain and
I know I should dodge you like murder
But it's things I shouldn't have that I crave I've
Never wanted things that were easy or
Good for me but if I did I'd probably pound
A stake through your chest yet

I've been meaning to tell you
How much I value the random moments
When you expose your helplessness to me,
When you peel back your ribs, show
Your heart swollen with misery and mystery
It spills out in bucketfuls like wine it
Makes me think down beneath it all you
Know rage is warm but love
Is the only fire that burns
Which I'm sure you'd never admit

Or want to hear and
I might not know much but I know
Love scares you more than the dark
Does little girls which is why
You have opened my coffined heart, you
Stand between me and my next breath and

Danielle, I've been meaning to tell you
But all the times I tried we were in
Some schmaltzy restaurant or someplace uncomfortable or
The words clotted like a cinderblock in my throat so
I've even thought about writing
But it's never worked once the pen was in my hand
I couldn't decide where to start or
What to say or the few words that I managed
Were tossed among the pile of papers on my floor
Besides, I really don't think I could finish it
Because then what would I do with it

Because Danielle, I've been meaning to tell you
But I doubt that I ever will.

SISTER JADE INSOMNIAC AND I

Found each other out of boredom
And the quest for new trouble in our lives
We grew up certain there'd been some mistake
That left us living in our state, terminally
Stuck like tourists who'd been lured
Into a red-necked white-assed male muck
Of a town before reaching our destination
It was clear as uncut meth
That we'd overstayed our welcome,
So we clung to each other like criminals
And behaved much the same
Crashing the parties of rich boys
And scratching chrome off their cars
There were times we wanted so desperately to escape
We probably needed an act of God
But bought a quarterbag instead
Then again, Sister Jade Insomniac and I
Have always played our problems
Like grand pianos
Played our problems
Like cacophonous lullabies
Whenever she's around I hear ambulance sirens
My little speedcrazed daredevil
We shed our skins and left the South
But sleep is still a place where we rarely go
We just sit around, sipping Molotov cocktails
From styrofoam cups
Swishing the taste of death
Around in our mouths,
Rolling it around on our tongues
Till we're drunk and we stumble
Into slurred sloppy heaps
Our bones might be drained of calcium
But they're packed to the joints
With disgust and discontent
We're like phantoms
That pace back and forth
Between fantasy and actuality

And our appetite for excitement is voracious
We live our lives without a safety catch
Because we're sick of society
Trying to shove us in its straightjackets
And rub our noses in its shit
We'd rather ride the rapids of quicksilver night
Right up till the time they
Evaporate, get sucked dry by dawn
And as the strange silence of morning
Closes in on us like a tomb,
I know she and I are coffined by this life
We're so eager to claw our way out of,

Our fingers ache

CONVERSATION WITH WHAT ONCE WAS A FRIEND

"Hey man, long time no see. You know, I was just thinking about you the other day, not 'cause of your message."

"Wait, which message do you mean? I didn't get any message, I swear. My roommate Tonya's kind of sketched-out you know, she's got this freaky boyfriend who's like been crashing at our place for months now and he's a really gnarly spaced-out '70s hangover who reeks of mildew and patchouli. I can't get over the fact that, like, they have sex and everything I mean I try to pretend it doesn't happen but sometimes they're so loud I have to stay at Jennifer's which kind of sucks because some of Jennifer's clients are housecalls and even though she says that's no biggie I really know I'm in the way which bites 'cause Rick is totally in my way and it's not like he fucking puts a dime out for rent but still you know I love Tonya to death so it's still cool and everything.

"I mean, I guess Rick's not that bad except that some of my stuff is missing and I don't want to jump to conclusions but last week I caught him going through my CDs just like seconds after he was bitching about how he was flat broke and then later when I got in from work there were gaps in spots where CDs were and I caught him shooting up in the bathroom and - get this - when I asked if he mopped me for a fix he just laughed and in a smacked-out voice said that I was paranoid and shouldn't freak and maybe he was right but coincidences are coincidences, you know?

"Plus I think he's been totally cheating on Tonya but I guess you can't exactly call it cheating 'cause I think they might have agreed to an open relationship or something. I mean, they were never like married or anything and monogamy is kind of weird because of Tonya's job but still

I think Rick's a slime. I mean, could you ever trust him? Oh, I forgot. You haven't met him but you'd hate his guts for sure and it's different if Tonya gets with people 'cause she does it to make a living for both of them so that's far from cheating, it's like a total separation of mind and body which I know probably sounds a bit corny 'cause I used to think the same thing till Tonya and I started doing dildo shows when we work the playpen which I promised myself I wouldn't do when I started stripping but loosened up 'cause that's the only way dancers make bank and besides, it's no big deal once you realize it's just acting.

"I mean, the customers are so sleazy sometimes I have to bite my tongue to keep from laughing but usually I just feel sorry for them 'cause they're not even human but then again I'm not even me when I'm up on the stage with all those calloused hands, moist bills of dead presidents, and gawking eyes scattered around in the dark sea beneath my spotlight where I just shake it and smile as if I wouldn't be anywhere else and they shuck out wads of cash in waves like some barter to make them believe it. I'm kick-ass convincing when I'm in work mode which basically is the way everybody has to be with the job scene. You know, that whole ass-kissing bit.

"In all types of jobs it's the same whether it's metaphorically or like the real thing 'cause work is what we do so we can be ourselves on our own time so I guess in a way we're all prostitutes but still I don't want you to think I'm a whore or anything 'cause I'm not a fucking whore and I'd never even consider degrading myself like that but the funny thing is I got four hundred bucks the other night just for beating the shit out of some sick old fucker who wanted Tonya and a dom to pair up for a fetish scene which was just a one-time thing that totally doesn't count because it's not like I actually had sex and not only that but I knew Tonya needed me to go along as a favor which was easier than I ever imagined 'cause all it came down to was a game of tug-of-war only with adults playing and not only that but a wrinkled-up wimp of an adult who paid a ton of money so he could lose and anybody who wouldn't go through with a deal like that is nuts which you can't even call it a deal 'cause it's not like I hooked the streets to set it up or anything and besides, it's not like I'll ever do it again 'cause I only needed the money so I could get back on my toes after that disappearing CD thing where I had to replace most of my favorites but since I decided I'm gonna kick after I finish up the last bit in my quarter it'll be no time till I have lots of extra cash which means I can relax and enjoy life a lot more.

"But it's not like I used enough that it was a problem or anything and nobody could ever peg me as a junkie which is why it totally bugs when people try to throw shade or guilt-trip me yet I'm still fully in control. I mean, I know tons of people say that type of thing even when they're way bummed-out and bananas but I wouldn't say something like that unless I knew it were true.

"I mean, remember when we took Philosophy together back in college and the main topic Dr. Schmidt always made a big deal about was the importance of personal integrity to the soul? I mean, that totally stuck with me and oh, that's rad you just got your degree. I'm sure I'll go back someday soon but that whole scene is more stress than I could handle right now and besides, it's not even practical anymore 'cause there are like, millions of people who graduate with honors and stuff yet they still end up slinging patties at McDonalds which is a nightmare I can't imagine even though it's totally my type of luck.

"But that's great that things are working out for you; I mean, I know I suck about getting in touch and stuff but that's just 'cause I get sidetracked a lot from being so hella busy that I barely have time to breathe but that doesn't mean you're not still like one of my favorite people in the world and I know we'll be friends forever and we're so close it doesn't matter if we don't talk for weeks, well, okay, months or whatever. Still it's no biggie 'cause we completely relate to each other and I'm jacked I got to see you today.

"Too bad I'm late and need to meet someone but we'll have to hang out sometime soon so we can act like old fogies and get all sloppy and sentimental about the old days even though it's silly to reminisce because it's not like things have changed so I guess we'll play up the whole sentimental game, you know kind of like when kids play doctor and fully get into it by acting like it's the most serious thing in the world and have a blast because they know it's not but nobody spoils the secret. That'd be killer to do with the sentimentality bit because old ninnies always feel the need to force emotional moments and stuff so they can, like, establish that whole times-have-changed-remember-when thing to make their friendship sacred. We can have fun and do a takeoff on all that since we know there's no point in slobbering over good-old-days stuff 'cause it's not like anything has changed. I mean, nothing's changed at all."

TO PUSH AWAY OR CLUTCH

Stanis and I were sprawled out on the uncomfortable prickly mess Jason tried to pass off as carpet, our backs pressed into what felt like colossal toothbrush bristles but that sticky October evening we couldn't have cared less, the taste of summer lingering in the backs of our mouths like the aftertaste of charcoal-filtered vodka and orange juice screwdrivers we'd been mixing in our mouths since the second we showed up at Jason's attempt at a party but was nothing more than an extra *ordinary* collection of loudmouthed small town kids lounging around with personalities as predictable as the black eyeliner, teased hair, Bauhaus t-shirt formula they shared for looking dark and mysterious, only since that was supposed to be a special event they were trying their damnedest, sporting shopping mall replicas of thrift store clothes crammed into Jason's $165-a-month attic apartment chainsmoking clove cigarettes and trying to hide when they coughed, speaking with bogus British accents as if that'd hide their boring American backgrounds based on beef jerky, bong hits, and microwave burritos.

To entertain ourselves, Stanis and I created a drinking game in which we took shots each time we heard a reference to Anne Rice novels, graveyards, tragic childhoods, or the expressions "killer" and "intense" so it should come as no surprise we were sloshed and obnoxious, laughing and taking bites from the exceedingly soggy slice of tragically hip and misunderstood as they fought for attention, any sense of importance, but then I saw him standing in the corner scraggly dark hair tossed around his shoulders onto the walls in messy strands, graffiti-tickling gaunt faces of models, perfect and magazine glossy. He inhaled a short forever from his cigarette and smiled at me with black eyes narrowed into slits. I felt myself ignite like the Marlboro cherry dangling from the end of his lips once I realized he was watching us watching them his jaw cocked sure and randy snicker curled in the corners of his mouth as if he was in on a big secret which actually he was, 'cause like the expression goes, you can't bullshit a bullshitter. I'd heard it from Stanis at least a million times so when he whispered, "Uh-uh, red flag, stay the hell away," that made Michael all the more desirable. He stepped across the room and stepped into my life, stepped all over obligatory small talk about how he'd seen me around or he thought I looked pretty cool or have I ever heard of the band...?

Instead I got to know him through the stories he told about his fetish for breaking into rich people's homes: hanging out, kicking back with big screen t.v.s and expensive wines till the police or security service would show then he'd hide in a closet or behind a tapestry, beneath a bed, listen to 'em boast about nothing wrong and all their restoring order shit which usually was his cue to zap 'em with his cattle-prod stun gun. None of that handheld miniature bit, he owned a magic wand that could clean a room with the flick of a wrist. He never stole a thing without a couple of uniforms flopping around on the floor in shock-spasms 'cause that's what made it fun, just like when he was wired on cheap Hell's Angels crank and snagged somebody's Alfa Romeo just so he could take it apart and scatter pieces all over Little Rock. He thought it'd make a great insurance report. He made life sound like a game he rewrote as he whisked across its board in a whirlwind, surviving alone, spinning smack-dab in the eye of independence. He seemed sexy and streetwise and tough without sounding stupid which excited me so greatly I could barely contain myself.

We bailed Jason's sinking ship of a social event and headed back to my place where we tiptoed through the door's emergency exit and marked the start of our deep and meaningful Gen-X post-John Hughes apocalyptic romance. Stanis sort of disappeared from the scenery during that three-week stretch. I didn't have time to hang out with him when I was busy smuggling bananas, boxes of cereal, and anything else from the cafeteria I could find to keep Michael from starving. I'd sit around and wait when he'd slither late-night through my dorm's window and scale the wall without a simple goodbye, which struck me as strange and poetic in a very '90s way as I wondered if I'd ever see him again, if he'd get shot in a fight with some gang, o.d. on smack he scored off the street, get thrown in jail to rot. By the time he'd saunter back to my room, my stomach and nerves were crushed up like aluminum cans which usually kept me from class but as soon as I saw him, I did my best to act nonchalant: recycle a sigh of relief with his steel kiss, remind myself he probably knows no other way, must've known nothing else in the past he told me next to nothing about. I was sure it was hell though. Somebody must've loved him at some point.

At that time I thought I did which is why once I stepped with him into the night, white tattered t-shirt on his back, a beacon that led me over fences, through alleys, around playgrounds, backyard pools. I tagged along the trail he tore just tight enough that he didn't notice me behind, pad in my pocket in case I needed notes about his secret ways of crime. I followed, sure he was leading me down a path of danger more intense than anything I'd thought or heard about. I was starving for excitement, so hungry for a bite strands of saliva hung from my mouth but at trail's end was no pot of gold but a stucco home the color of dried tuna, a front door Michael opened by key rather than screwdriver or stolen credit card, floodlights in a constellation that came to life when I moved towards a window, trying to peek through its slats.

I was lit on display on the well-trimmed grass, framed for Michael's mother, a chubby lady who popped outside like some sort of parent-in-a-box, a blaze of fuzzy blue nightgown fury, her face contorted in disgust as she screamed about how I should be ashamed poking around on their private property; she'd had enough of snotty-nosed brats, ill-bred punk rockers and democrats like me being bad influences on her sweet little

Mikey, keeping him out to God-awful hours of the a.m. and causing him to get bad marks at school and detention - just what was I trying to prove anyway, bullying her sweet baby? I stood speechless, the situation making no sense till I found out he was seventeen. I didn't know what to say so I watched the sweat shine on her cheeks, mounds of flesh which shook as she rambled, flapped as she screeched, her mouth an opened map to a world of PTA meetings, baloney sandwiches, gospel choirs, and country crafts as common to him as to me.

That reckless little wanna-be streetsmart daredevil - he slid into my life like a soft whisper but faded to a dull outline, a stretched-out shadow lingering inside his mother's home. He watched her bring the truth to life, watched her watching me smile about the things I learned he wasn't: mysterious, powerful, mean. And as I turned and walked away, grinning wider, still I loved him most for what he was: a scared boy trying to hide behind a leather jacket and look tough.

He never came around again. I haven't seen him since. Still some nights thoughts of him keep me awake: the times we shared within a slot when neither of us was sure of much of anything. Wrapped tight in college, the world of make-believe, just as it starts to seem real to me again suddenly it's morning and I wake to milky bright sunlight gushing through the windows, waves from my loud alarm clock rippling throughout my bare apartment. No furnishings of Michael, Stanis, no traces of Jason to be found. The only things to push away or clutch, a wad of cold sheets on my bed.

THE TRUTH ABOUT MODELING

The air is brittle and cold as
I stand on this pedestal, undressed
And exposed like an old crime confessed,
Secrets I have no longer. The instructor has
Put on music for our comfort, jazz
From her jam box. Still I tremble, body caressed
By the gaze of strangers, let my thoughts digress
From this situation as
Much as possible. With time I might
Become comfortable with this job, these students
In the studio staring at me. Technique they are taught,
And technique I learn, too, though not quite
The same. Mine is the art of being prudent,
Hiding shame, for Donatello's David I am not.

WINNER

Some people talk about the 'old school' but baby, I'm the *only* school and I'm so 15 minutes ahead it *hurts*. I've got a vision for the future and its tracking is so tight, it blows that 20/20 bullshit away in a warpspeed whirlwind of flimsy cardboard optometrist charts with their universe-*ago* universal letter E's as headings, E standing for elementary but I've passed post-secondary, mastered Masters, nursed a few Doctorates to health with my even-newer-and-newest sight explained in layman's terms as 20/.0000001 and when I say 'Layman,' it's as in *laying*, as in stagnant but I'm all supraluminal evolution about it. I'm the after-aftermath of Gen X 'cause I'm not about to genuflect and X is just another variable or ancient orthodox Christ symbol or somethin' whereas I'm all Post-Post-Everything which is even Post-Nothing before it becomes a *something*, and whatever it is I already call *was* 'cause I was over it before it even began. I'm the overdeveloped underexposed high-tech hypothesis for an ultra-stimulated information-laden hyper-hyphenated culture. I'm the postscript to the afterthought to the epilogue of history's story when it went from his story to the politically-correct his-and-her story to the politically-*corrected* his-and-her multifaceted multicultural mega-translated story without regard to race, color, class, sexual orientation, types of food ingested, drug use or abuse, physical capabilities or creed. I've transcended that whole scene: archetypes and archetypal archetypes and the form of Plato's philosophy of the omniscient omnipotent ever-present allegedly unattainable forms. I ran the human race and won and all I've lost is me.

PARTLY CLOUDY

Flouncing About

like a spotlit
cartoon, he's a moment he's

a move-
ment of the slack-

jawed smooth
syllabled character he becomes

spouting carefully oiled
phrases out eleven p.m. dead

alive and half awake enough
to brush his teeth with crystal

meth with entourage of
gnats and flies for a fan Club

Boy flexes a smile wide
as a billboard shiny

synthetic and white as asbestos
stirred up, mainlined

prepped right
out of the can because

life is like a
bare-boned rig, he

says so
he'll just grit his

teeth and take it, fake
it till he makes it: Club

Boy's latest con-
versation with mirrors, his bulls-

eyed pupils breathe tales of old
friends smeared together, strangers

now as he looks
at himself foam green some

preface with "sea" color-
coordinated clothing and feels

like a bad trans-
lation his expression

hangs like a prisoner in
the bathroom's cadaverous

silence a
growling throb in

the back of his
throat across

a filmy Aqua
Net hairsprayed ex-

panse staring at
this molded plastic

torso why
am I here? he asks

what am I
doing? but in comes

a falsetto cloud of
queens and on blares

the music the
lullaby of small talk, gossip

and complaints he
tickets a Long Island Tea the

answer sticks in
his frigid

sublet flesh no
way to squint away

how much is real how
much is calculated

for effect

PAINED AND PAINTED

she slices the dance-
floor's skin with grace executed

smooth as an angel blade's flick;
grenades in her head and she's about to blow

cigarette smoke and sweat perfume
the air heavy against her

face bleached blank and shiny, like a wax
doll's. Faraway eyes should

've been dead by dawn, Club Girl's
a fixture with jittery foundation

she stands poised at the edge, arm
extended with a nuclear pink

cocktail balanced between slender fingers
fresh from the bar's harlot throated first

call, a soft rolling of
the skull and brittle yellow

stalks of hair tumble a-
cross her

trademark hair
tossing gesture to dis-

guise an inventory glance to-
night she's featuring her latest fierce waif

diva incarnation, an update debuted
through her custom cut icy

white supatex dress, complete
with latex/patent leather platform

boots, shiny black
plasticene adhesive eyelashes long

as her list of lovers, eyes
helmeted by aquamarine colored

contacts the ghost
impressions of her hang

over seconds between a
kind of time lapse photography which

vomits who she used

to be what she Club
Girl is

not she
speaks through clenched

jaws and a sugar frosted smile
drops names and promises and

pills from her hip pocket into
conversation friends

flimsy as a movie set this
stage of world she

keeps her secrets up
past the night's elastic

stars

DRESSED TO THE TEETH

I have tired of my face pressed
to the windowpane staring watching
waiting gazing at this bloody month
of winter unwinding itself before me
pumping lost love letters and
lipstick stains on private parts
in its flow I
have tired
of it
I am tired
so I shamelessly step
from a life lived by
scrupulous selection into
the apocalyptic fury
outside inside: a
cinematic panshot
the remains of myself given over
to frosty pink lipglossed hookers skirting
about in see-through blouses and
micro spandex wrappers slit
to the curve of ass cheeks jiggling in
twenty-five dollar anticipation of
some john who'd like a snack to eat
I'm the only one who seems to
be paying either attention or them
and I want to brush my teeth
brushing off a Suzy Wrong with
a flyspecked complexion who
can barely speak English
pleading "you want sucky-
fucky?" and poking her
chopsticked fingers at me
my boots shuffle by
dry on chipped concrete the
sidewalk cracks resembling dark
veins lonely for someone's teeth

I make it to my fluorescent-
lit mailbox and
laugh as if I'm mocking
the whole codependent
romantic notion, trying to
pretend I don't know damn
well that yesterday's date
was February thirteenth
Valentine's Day licks its
vampire chops and
drools ropes of red tar like
severed arteries
my stomach churns with
nervousness as I stick
my mailbox with the stake-
shaped key and twist
and turn and
peek inside its
guts there's
an offering of a single
crimson-colored
square piece of paper which
I yank out like an abortion
and head back across
the street toting
the casket of red death
beneath my arm and
grinning shit at the call girls' hissing
"Here, kitty kitty" my
thoughts are frisky - frenzied and
distant my heart races with
all the possibilities of an empty-
cornered envelope
the intoxication of remembrances
an address to return to and
memories to address
with an abbreviated
version of a smirk curled
in the corners of my mouth
I shove my thumbnail unseal
pry but what I find

inside yanks my tongue
out and smashes
my ribcage from the
impact of that pot-bellied bastard
cupid sprawled out on
a generic greeting card
the message "I've got an eye
on your sweet tooth, Valentine"
streamlined in the shape of
an arrow and "Best Wishes
from Dr. Stepka, d.d." some-
thing-or-other down
at the bottom the
sweet slogan in script letters
words that
curl and close themselves
around me:
all my living breathing something
turning nothing, empty-
gutted like last year's
heart-shaped cardboard box,
a shell that once housed
chocolate treats now
graveyard of past lovers and friends
packed to the hilt
I stiffen with the ghostlike
reminder that love
is a noose
dimly or definitely or
disguised like
those letters of "Best
Wishes..." are lies
in peppermint-colored curlicued drag
to drag a sucker in but
then again I've
never even cared about
the trumped-up sweetheart
scene, always have known that
bit is
no disease for me
I head towards my

place, cut out
scissor-stepping hard and
brisk and cold
a rapid streak so
quick I can't unveil or even see
the emptiness of dark mascara-
clustered eyes surrounding couldn't
can't be anything
like me
I step
feel the whirring of flared nostrils
step and
force a smile
I step
sway my arms as if I've got snake-
eyes beneath my sleeves
because being sincere
solves nothing
I step and
step and make
it to my stoop and
solve my problem of the moment
by leaving it behind
Valentine's Day a past
now passed
shot down like
this gunpowder night that
sighs with its
softbound sounds from the gutter
wheezes coughs and
spits out a silt-
stained backdrop for
a crumbling city
St. Valentine's a
myth forgotten a
false belief outgrown
like training bras or hopes
for true love treadmarked
by the sole of my shoes
that step
I step and

for a second before I kiss
the delusion smack dab on the lips,
I am afoot with
reaching my remembrances
dressed to the teeth
in fabulous
                    vacancy

PANHANDLED PRESENCE

At the bus stop last week (at least
I think it was) my balance was thrown off
before a skeezy Sixth and Market
not–so-delicate deli
where a woman unwound herself
like some wild-eyed hurricane, springin'
clinky-slinky forth and flingin'
bloody chunks of teeth at me
"Heeeeey there ma'am," she said,
"I know ya got's some change
Ya got's t'have some change fer me,"
scorching my cheeks with her breath, its
stench like a decade of stale beer
"Nope, sorry," I lied and shook my head
with a slow-motion shift of discomfort
like bare thighs against a vinyl carseat
her greasy gaze, Silly Putty colored skin
sticking to me
eyes glazed over like naugahyde
"Woo Hoooo! Well, well, *well*,"
she said, looked me up and down and
then spat out a laugh and a
dark yellow lung creature that
clung to her lips as she spattered
stared stuttered stammered
"Ain't *you* a sight, Miss Thing,
all gussy-ass hussied up!
Prancy boy, prancy boy
Didn't thought ya was a dude,"
and slung her fingers 'round in the air
like runaway dumplings
mouthin' "C'ain't 'spect *nuthin'*
from no faggoty drag queen."
I wasn't even wearing makeup
yet I'd still been cast the part
the whole routine was so freaky

it made me think of my friend
Desiree, not because she's a freak
(even if she's been described as
a 'Psychoses Variety-Pack: Family Size')
but 'cause she views her life as a movie
and it seemed
that's what mine had become
I just stood there, wondering
"Okay, do I get cue cards now, or what?"
wishing someone would fast-forward to the credits
and take me back to reality
somebody somewhere pushed a button, I suppose
the bus arrived
but like the trite expression goes,
"Be careful what you wish for"
I stepped inside and
got a heapin' helpin' of reality
the doors sealed themselves tight
and I was on the bus alone
except that her words had stuck to me
like suicide
and they were real
I was trapped in terminology
and it was very real
Prancy Boy, Prancy Boy

reality's a tale that's curled
at the edges
and its tracking is tight,
volume cranked loud
blasting out clichés
one-step solutions and tommyrot talk
reality's a tale told by chapped lips
of teenage Polk Street boys
whistlin' Dixie and suckin' dicks
behind the five-and-dime
for twenty dollars
reality's the dark and vaporous shadow
that lurks in
San Francisco's neon rainbow flag
spread across the skyline like a welcome mat

for the world's largest outpatient program
a place where you can get your own freedom,
buy your own Freedom Rings
reality's the awful truth that hides within the pride:
that 'freedom' can also own you,
leave you labeled, lined up on the shelf
with all the other Castro lies for sale
shrinkwrapped and packaged 'K-Tel Presents:
The Latest and Greatest Pink Triangle Hits'
and aren't those damaged songs
complete rip-offs
cheap pastel-sounding jingles
where everybody kisses and makes up
and life's a carefree smiley-faced card
because that's the way it is,
and that's just the way things are,
that's why.
Oh, what glorious freedom
what slavery in drag
the same language that's been dressed up
is the one that holds you down
pinned and mounted in suspended sentences
limp-cock talk of who's a 'bottom,'
who's a 'top'
for the sake of everyday uselessness
smothered by blanket statements
Prancy boy, Prancy boy

"Cryin's for sissies. Hush up and be a man."
    translated to
"Cryin's for wimps. Bend over and take it like a man."
        scenery changed from
"Act straight or get your ass kicked."
    to
"Act straight or your ass gets no dick."

Prancy boy, Prancy boy
trapped tight in the gaze of my peers
and those who peer at me
I feel the hunger of their blank stares
their smiles sneers whispers stifled giggles forced conversations

any each and every something
expecting everything, offering nothing
I break into a tight-lipped smile
to keep from breaking, push salutations and small talk
through the spaces between my teeth
as if I'm some fuckin' jack-o-lantern
empty-gutted and illuminated with
fabulous vacancy
act so happy it makes me wanna puke tuna casserole
'cause if I don't, people say that I'm bitter
they say I'm bitter
and I'd rather be bitter than bullshit
but since I know there's no glory road to salvation,
no glory hole to gratification,
I guess I should just take things as they are
Prancy boy, Prancy boy
C'aint 'Spect   Nuthin'
just take things
when what I'd really rather say is, "Heeeey
baby, I know ya got's some change
Ya got's t'have some change fer *me*."

Funny Again

and I laugh and
hear my smile as it sticks
against teeth it's
half past get up in the morning
and I've been blasted
out of sleep a
distorted rendition of
Salt and Pepa's "Push It" dances
through my radio alarm
dressed in static and
the sound of my telephone as it rings
ringing ding a ling lingering
throughout this skull too soft to
greet the outside world
head on I
remain thinly veiled behind
answering machine and
listen as its throat stretches out
in what sounds like a test of
the emergency broadcast system
much more than a beep which
is somewhat ironic since
the caller leaves no message I
suppose the emergency is
me

I don't want to get up don't
want to face the bathroom
mirror's reflection I
wish I were wrapped tight in
blankets and pleasant dreams
instead of this tight-
featured tight-lipped
reality of being
something dangerous is

inside my smile it's
more sinister than before
I started getting finger-fucked
by the Jack Frost of things
I used to think I'd want
but never expected to find
just like deep in the woods
behind my parents' home:
cottonmouths
soft yella-bellied twisters
they were always waitin'
sunbathin'
their slender bodies
spread out in the weeds
along paths beaten
by my childhood friends
and me

cotton-
mouths like
wartime snipers little
diamond-eyed death machines
barely movin' or breathin'
layin' low for an
attack the
chance to slide and
spread their poison
their chiseled jaws like
set traps

my mom was terrified of them, in
fact I heard about them from
her first "you must always proceed
with caution and must never
second-guess" she said
"any place as if at any
given time you should expect
to find one there"
one popsicle-sticky afternoon
when I was either nine or ten I
found out what they look like in the

flesh so to speak for
myself my mom
was with me I was with
her grocery shopping when
we chanced upon a traveling sideshow act
right there in the Harvest Foods parking lot
where mom sifted through spare change and
counted out fifty cents a pop to
a potbellied geezer who flashed his collection of
fuzzy orange-sweatered teeth, stubs the
tips of which were sharpened to faded
yellow points so precisely they resembled
candy corn as he smiled and
stepped aside a gesture granting our admission
through the Winnebago's aluminum door
inside a weathered brown bag of an old man
stood from his fold-out lawn chair soon as
he saw us and prodded each sleeping pile of serpents
awake with a shove of his rake behind the
speckled glass pane separating us and themselves
one of them from what we learned was
the venomous pile had to be shaken loose from
his big stick as if on cue my mom's
arm shot in front of me
her body a very visible shiver at the sight of how
the snake angrily unwound when thrown back
to the shimmering mass in a thick lazy slap
which I began to resemble soon most my
middle school days with the frustrated way I'd slump
down in my seat when in class

senior year of college I began
to prepare my big getaway from
the South
juggled three jobs got
up mornings six a.m.
even when it wore me thin 'cause
I knew I had to get out
I'd had more than my share of settling for
spitfire serpent kisses and that
lame striptease act so

graduation day I took off bust or CA
wavin' goodbye with my middle finger and
spittin' dust Hell on Wheels in a U-Haul
I shed 23 years of dusty roads, Ro-Tel dip, and
sharing my bedsheets and sex
with golden-skinned good ol' boys always at
the brink of shedding me
or sinking in their teeth

I knew there had to be somethin'
else knew I had to find knew there surely
must be anything somewhere else
so to the Bay Area I made my way
fat-faced and full of promise
jonesin' for somethin' to jump-start my heart,
send it pumping what I discovered
instead was San Fransissy life at
breakneck speed why this
city doesn't come with a warning label
still's a mystery to me
slide yourself into and beneath
it feel the fierce way desire
tourniquets itself around you and
clings

Clubland South of Market tweak-
chic trannies powder their noses from
bullet-shaped compacts and flick their forked
tongues like switchblades as they burn the night
down bleed day to night to day to

Mission sidestreets where pythons hide
twenty dollar balloons beneath their tongues which
get bartered in smiles quicker than a coke buzz and
tossed out through the cracks

cottonmouth kisses
camouflage emotions and
strike with a vengeance
when he
wants and she

wants and they
want and I
won't

Genet was right, I suppose
when he wrote "The only way
to avoid the horror of horror is
to give in to it"
it's
the nature of
the economy of the
business it's the
nature of
things

the body of humanity
has been poisoned
it appeals to me
about as much as lukewarm oatmeal

I'm a whispering lullaby
I'm a crumpled-sleeve throwback
with rattle-tipped words and
bloodstained eyeteeth

my blood beginning to
grow cold, grow old
of all of this
shoulda been coulda been any-
thang somethin'
else

shoulda been coulda been
anything something
else

should've been could've been
anything, something
else

but ya know, I really should

be going hey but still we could
maybe get together this weekend I mean
this one but not this one necessarily really any-
time my schedule's open so
am I almost to almost to just about anything we'll have to well, not have
to have but would if we could yeah, we
should hook up sometime and do something

but the telephone is
trembling, desperate to
tell me some-
thing and we can
if we would what we
could and I
should've been yet
still some-
how it seems there's
always some-
thing I have
to do, and the
wet of these feelings is
dying like frozen breath
but there's some-
thing I have to do,
always something I
have to do al-
ways some thing I
have to
do

SPUN

I am powder
pressed tight and zip
locked in micro baggies
I am promises for
perfection and for
ever lined up blown
away or torn
like cotton
bandages
I am cut with
all the wrong
words and
fervent manic stirrings
wave the red flag
put up your caution
signs I
am dangerous
with my lab con-
structed wings and
the way I come
unhinged like a
screen door

TAKING CARE OF

I stand before the door, cataloging all the details I don't think I've ever noticed: the way the number 9 isn't aligned with the 1 and the 2 before it, a necklace of shallow gouges around the doorknob, dark lines in the wood like veins close to skin, small clusters of paint that are beginning to crack off. I scrape the faded beige color with my fingernail and watch it tumble to the floor in tiny flakes, wondering how I ever managed to edit my memory so flagrantly from the reality of what a dump this place is. I hold my breath, fearing that I'll inhale asbestos or some other carcinogen, as I knock on the door and come to the sudden conclusion it was stupid of me to return.

Rappety rap rap. My arms are at my side, and my heart seems to be beating with that same pattern, that same rappety rap rap. For a second, I wonder if I knocked at all or just imagined it, but then I hear rough rustlings of metal and the door is cracked open before me. Michael peeks his head around it, his dark hair spilling to the side.

"Vic! I haven't seen you in... I mean, how's it going?"

His voice wavers and he takes a step back, peeling off this barrier between us swiftly as a band-aid on an old wound. I glance behind him, quickly scanning the clutter of his apartment. I notice it looks much dirtier than I remember it. I notice the drawing he did of me is no longer on the wall.

"D'ya want to come in?" he asks, extending his hand into the space which once was ours. I nod and force a smile, stepping forward, despite my impulse to turn and run. I feel like an idiot for being here; I feel I should give him some sort of explanation.

"I was just in the neighborhood," I lie, looking at cracks in the concrete and half-laughing at my corny use of cliché, "and I wanted to see how you're doing." I walk down the hall towards the living room, and I wonder if that's why I'm really here. I want to believe it is, since I don't have a valid reason. I feel lost, curious, nervous, displaced. In fact, the entire scenario seems awkward. I stop at the entrance to the living room and stand immobile, listening as he shuts the door and locks it.

"You've always been anal about that," I mutter, thinking about the time he freaked out because I left the door open when I'd gone to check the mail.

"Huh?" I feel him walk and stand beside me, though I don't have the nerve to look.

"Oh, nothing," I say, staring at my absence on the wall. The only picture still hanging is a Scotch-taped Polaroid taken when he was in Mexico, that vacation he used to refer to incessantly. "I was just saying it's been a long time."

"Yeah, it has. A really long time."

Then I force myself to look into his eyes, shuddering at the contact with reminders that I shouldn't have. After all the preparation I've done, all my attempts to overcome him, his eyes still entrance me. They're dark and glossy. Mysterious. Mesmerizing. I don't want to have to stop looking at them, even though I know they don't see me the way they once did. It bothers me to think how they see me now, a stranger in this new world of his.

Michael notices that I'm gawking at him and he looks away. "Sorry the place's such a wreck," he says in what seems like a polite attempt. "You know I've never been the June Cleaver type."

I observe the landscape of laundry strewn about the room in mounds, the crusty-edged dishes in precarious stacks, and deduce that he's single. He doesn't have a live-in lover, at least — two people couldn't possibly occupy a space where so much junk is piled up.

"Aw, it's not too bad," I say. "Not bad at all, in comparison to mine."

He continues to avoid eye contact with me, slowly scanning his room as if expecting to find some change in scenery; then scuttling off to the kitchen with his abrupt change of mind.

"D'ya want anything to drink?"

"No thanks. I'm fine," I answer, not quite certain about the words.

"Really? Not even a glass of juice or anything? I'm so parched, I could just die."

Juice. "Well... orange juice doesn't sound too bad. If you've got it, that is," I say, remembering that he usually keeps a gallon-size container in his fridge.

"Sounds good to me, too," he calls from the kitchen, his voice bouncing off the linoleum. "So, what's been going on?"

"Going on? Oh, you know, eating, sleeping, working... all the thrills and chills of life."

Silence.

"Still working as an English tutor?" he asks.

"Unfortunately. I'm afraid it'll never end. I expected to find something else by now."

"Yeah, I remember when you were hired for the job you said you didn't want it to be permanent." I hear the refrigerator door shut with a sucking noise; then he returns to the room, a large glass in each hand.

"Here you go," he says, smiling. "Y'know, you're welcome to have a seat."

"Oh. Thanks." I maneuver myself around the plates and glasses and plop down on the recliner. "I've always loved this chair."

I feel a bit comfortable now. I'm comfortable, and I'm glad that I've come here. After all the time we invested in one another, there isn't any reason why we shouldn't be able to get along. We can still be friends. We can do this.

"I know it's kind of weird that I showed up here," I say. "But I like it."

"Yeah? You do?" He stands with his arms loosely crossed.

"Yeah. It should've happened long ago, but I don't think I was ready yet. I had to get things into perspective."

"Always a good thing to do."

"Yeah."

"That's all I ever wanted, you know."

"Yeah, I know. It took me a while, but I've got it all together now." I notice that I'm nodding my head and I wonder how long I've been doing it. Attempt to be cool, I think. You can do this.

"Great," he says, pushing a pile of papers off the couch. They tumble over one another like sheets in a dryer, only they're being tossed all over the floor. A few of them land on the dishes beside me, and I make out that they're new sketches of his. He plops down without even bothering to glance where they've landed and nonchalantly sips his orange juice. He still has that charm, that unaffected grace I've always loved.

I'm eager to step into his world again. "What have you been working on?" I ask, positioning the glass between my legs and leaning over the arm of the chair. I pick up one of the pieces before he has a chance to answer. It's a pastel drawing of a devil whispering in an angel's ear. The angel's eyes are wide with consternation and one of his hands is covering his mouth. "Promises, Promises" is written across the top of the page in a crimson scrawl resembling gashed flesh. I look at the letters and think of how we used to listen to that song late at night while he sat on the couch the way he is now, and a series of mental pictures begins to flash before me: the stiff-backed pose Michael had me model for my portrait, the time we made love and Michael knocked over a cup filled with paint-polluted water and stained the wad of clothes beside us. My vision is clouded with Michael, Michael, Michael.

"This is excellent," I say, putting the piece back on the floor and picking up a charcoal study he did of hands. I reposition myself and a little bit of the orange juice spills on my crotch, but I choose to ignore it.

"Thanks." He seems unaffected. I wonder if his apathy is real or a facade. I wonder if he misses me, if he ever wakes up in the middle of the night and resists an urge, an impulse to call me, the way that I do with him.

I delicately place the charcoal drawing on an open patch of his floor and tell him that I wish he'd take better care of his works. "After all," I say, "they're fantastic."

He shrugs. "That doesn't really matter to me. The important thing is that I release everything, get it out. Once I deal with those emotions, I don't need them anymore. They're taken care of, you know? And that's what's important to me, not the product."

Not the product. I take a sip of juice and feel it slide down my throat, recognizing this explanation he has given me many times in the past. This time, I finally hear what he tried to tell me long ago. The important thing for him is the sense of a release, not the product. Not the product. Not. The. Product.

I don't feel very comfortable here after all. In the span of a few seconds, he's disturbed the past as I knew it, stolen the truth as I thought it was, reduced over two years of our life to rubbish. I never expected to find him tenaciously clinging to memories of the time we spent together, but I also didn't think his emotions were based solely on immediacy: what's comfortable today, what eliminates his worries, his tension. As I sit here in the apartment once again, I can't help but notice the path of pictures on the floor, and I realize that they and I are the same: products he no longer needs, things of which he had rid himself.

Michael picks up the remote control from the arm of the couch and flicks on the t.v. Some typical program is on, and it's typically annoying: an overweight comedienne vulgarly pushing around her size and bitching about how much she hates the resurgence of paper-thin models. She claims they looked disgusting twenty years ago, so they definitely don't need to be updated now. "I mean, could you seriously date someone who only eats, like, three pieces of lettuce a day?" she asks the audience. Michael laughs, and I stare at him in disbelief. He's hunched over with his head rested on his hand, gawking as if the program is fascinating or something. Yeah, sure. There's no way that he could find this garbage entertaining. I know he doesn't care about the show; he just doesn't want to have to think about new topics, about what he should say to me next. It's not as if I'm quite into the art of conversation either, though. I think about my portrait instead, wondering if he would give it to me.

"Um, Michael, whatever happened to that..." I begin, gazing at all the white space on his wall, but then I stop. It doesn't seem to matter to me anymore. Blank is how I feel: blank about taking the effort to ask the question, blank about being in his apartment, blank about an old period of my life.

He doesn't look away from the t.v. "Happened to what?"

I pause, frantically thinking about a way to complete my sentence. "Old neighbor of ours, the crazy lady who thought that you and I stole her cat?"

"She's still around, I guess. I haven't seen her in a while, haven't thought to pay attention. Who cares, anyway?" He yawns and stretches his arms.

Oh please, I think, you don't have to do the whole I'm-so-bored-with-this-conversation bullshit. I'll be gone soon enough. In fact, I'm surprised that I haven't left yet. I don't know what I'm waiting on.

"I think I'm gonna get something to eat," he announces. "Want anything? I have some ice cream sandwiches and stuff."

"No thanks. I'm fine," I say, and I realize that I am. It dawns on me that this is why I came here: to feel fine, to wean myself of him once and for all. I may have been another product, I think, looking at him, but I don't need you anymore. I don't need to be fed by your attention or your ice cream bars. I don't need to try and relive the past. I don't need you, Michael.

He stands up, heads back into the kitchen, and begins shifting things about in his icebox. I wish that I could voice my thoughts. I know it's over; I can feel the distance, the stretch of space between us, and it doesn't seem to be a big deal.

"Mmm mmm. Hey, I forgot about these ice cubes I made out of Coke the other day. Cool, huh? You want any?"

"Coca-Cola ice cubes?" I push myself out of the recliner. "No, I'm not in the mood for anything sweet, really."

"Okay. Your loss," he says, forcing a friendly laugh. It disgusts me. I can't bear being in his presence another instant.

I walk over to the lone photograph of him in Mexico, rip it down, and head for the exit. No, your loss, I think, fumbling with the lock. I can hear him snapping ice cubes from their plastic tray and dropping them into a glass with a clink, clink, clink, clink as I storm down the stairs of the complex without bothering to close his door behind me or take one last look at the place.

I step onto the pavement outside and begin briskly walking in the early summer evening. "Okay, that's it," I say, working my way through pedestrians a bit slower than me. "I've done it."

The heat of August is oppressive, but I feel strong now, free. My feet keep moving and I impulsively toss the sweaty photo of Michael over my shoulder, pleased to finally experience a release, to rid myself of an unneeded product.

RUBAIYAT FOR ROCKY

Morning breaks. So do bottles and bones.
So does the face of a once small town boy with flesh tones
Ridged and scratchy as a crayon drawing
His eyes stained red and curtainless, two crimson-colored stones

Cast by virtue of his disarray.
His head pulls back like a plunger, a
Trick of toxic waters crashing in, another
Moment resolved the same lackluster way

Which used to make him feel
More excited than he really was. Now a dime-bag deal
Barely gets him out of bed; he's
Become the evil that's been fed i.v.-meals

To himself, by himself. The needle the
Tip the dull point, tools which would prove to be
His only friends, if there weren't also rituals to his
Addiction. Alone, he keeps these secrets. Few see

What lurks beneath his sleeves, the sleep-
Ing hollows of his arm: legends which deep
In the middle of lonely places – among scar
Tissue, bleach and water and blood – exist in whittled heaps.

iNky BLOATER

exhaust-fume blue eyes the
lustre of dry ice
hair black soot and mostly wet
like the lazy July air and
the drift into slow-water drugs
vampire that he was
he ran me up my first time
then plucked the raw red rosebud
where I'd been stuck by
lapping it up with his tongue
bullet-hole shot of smack and
I sat and stared at
the sandblasted ceiling
all twenty-two years of me
dully surprised when
the currents of chiva began
swishing through my veins
I'd read heroin horror stories
on and off and on again
in my teens and
had wondered if I could try it without
losing my life, leaving me
impaled by needles, forearms

crucified and

after all the times I'd thought
about it during late-night home therapy sessions
cursing myself as a virgin junkie
and rubbing my inner arms
instead of counting sheep

    I'd promised myself to keep far,
    far away, yet

that night
his room instead of mine
it took a strange slow motion moment to
hit me
    it had hit me
there,
right there inside me,
as near as
near could be.   a
series of shudders up
the spine   next
I heard him laugh, ask
me how I was.   I was
slumped at the edge of the bed
my
arms crossed my
eyes closed till
I forced them open to
see his series of words which
moved through the air like a trail of birds, formed
questions of "*Man, are you okay?*" and "*Hey,*
can you hear me? Can you hear me?" or what or what   or

what came next: a nudge, the slap of his palm
on my face   that stung   I
watched him lean over me, hair
spinning like a whirlwind as
he shook and he
shook him-
self   me   us
yelling, "*Hey are you okay are*
you okay are you-" those words,
words a trail of birds then
carrion

I opened my mouth to reply
but managed nothing more than
a short whimper he
somehow heard and
stopped screaming, put
his ear to my lips so

brittle and dry that
when I moaned the
bottom one cracked open
with a sound resembling the
crunch of boots against snow

a strand of saliva followed
he wiped the trickle off my chin

    strange   stranger:
pile of dead limbs that I was,
I smiled a junksick smile at him
ankles
        knees
                    hips
head   dumped across his bed
like unshelved books, a
menacing dark jumbled mess
that drifted into something
close to sleep

sprawled out on the mattress
my body a thick throbbing as
I barely peeked through slats
of what looked like shut lids
he stayed nearby his face sharp-
featured and slender eyes
inert as he surveyed his plate   soon
as he was certain that I
hadn't stopped breathing he
peeled off his long sleeves   put his
arm in position   tied off   found
a main vein   mainlined
then plopped down on his back
beside me   and with quivery
hands and fingertips proceeded
portioning the frazzle I'd been
worn to   into parts

my stomach rolled with nausea
fear   shock   beige wallpaper dying

targeted for the feed
that raven-haired boy whom
I'd met at a club
planned a 'nevermore' for me

loneliness written all over him
but
          his appetite curbed by
my serious nod and
a high still flowing from his inner arm
across gouged-out ridges of
ribs in a thin stream

a splash of sticky tongue
danced slow and vulgar across skin
I knew I couldn't afford another
minute of stay as
he tried to find my needle
flower again

I reached for a cigarette
blew the remainder of the
night we'd shared through
my teeth and
slid out of bed

          disappearing
like the violent-colored blemish

head
long into un-
scarred ebony arms

of night

AT THE EDGE

dull concrete
I crouch, almost
sit
cold
shallow end of a
stomach striped
deep indigo
slashes this
bleached blue monster
hurls back bent
faces
stares straight
through me and
laughs with chlorine breath

no, it
would not be
nice to
drown.

ALLEGORY

A blue blaze of color ignites, erupts behind my eyelids. In a blink, there's a strike of shocking blue; then a spasm of vibration that shudders up my spine and works its way into my inner ear. I hear a high-pitched ringing and notice a shift of equilibrium, a difference in the quality of space. Then I slip out of the seat I've been sharing with a young girl – her hair a bundle of black and copper braids that look like jumpropes – and slide past the scenery of San Francisco's public transportation, a mix of spices that range from street folk to senior citizens, from schoolkids in vinyl and fake-fur clothing as loud as their mouths to businessmen with lips pressed tight as their three-piecers. Their image stretches as I whiz by, drop right through the bottom of this tin can bus.

I close my eyes, blurry vision and the helpless feeling of falling too much for me to handle. But the sensation of plummeting stops as quickly as it started. I'm grounded by a tremendous thud and bolts of pain that crack across my shins, reverberate throughout my body. My eyes dart open, and I'm overwhelmed by the immediate sense of opening, of closing in, I notice as my vision adjusts to the change of environment. My surroundings have metamorphosed to massive brick walls in place of the bus's welded scrap metal, ornate stained-glass windows rather than smudgy fragile frames.

It dawns on me I've surfaced in a vast cathedral. Fear strikes my heart as I comprehend my complete loss of familiarity, of stability.

I struggle to find my breath. I'm smothered within a sea of nude bodies, a singular wet splotch that extends as far as I can see in every direction. Something in me loosens the gooseflesh of realization that I've somehow also been picked clean of my clothes. I feel as if a stroke of clumsiness whisked me away, reduced me to an anonymous fleck blending into the thousands of different fleshtones that bleed into each other.

My skin is slick with sweat from these strangers surrounding me, their oils lubrication on my undraped body. "Where the fuck am I? What happened to my clothes?" I hear myself cry, vulnerability swelling inside me. "What the fuck is going on?"

Nobody answers.

I don't like this situation at all. I flinch, shove with the weight of my body, but resistance defeats me. The most I can do is slide a few inches forward, backward, up and down, side to side. Extending my limbs is out of the question. The bodies pressed against me are pressed against bodies blocked by bodies crammed against bodies...

"*Hello?* Who are all of you? Do-"

My voice cracks. I pause, swallow.

"Does anybody speak English?" More frustrated: "Agh! Can anybody help at all?"

A few of them glance in my direction, respond to my pleas with turns of the head and murky black unblinking eyes, scary, like a shark's but nothing more. Yet these silent gestures speak volumes. The distant expression on their faces, long looks of exhaustion and indifference, tells me that they're past the point of caring about me, let alone how this scenario began or how it will end or really much of anything at all.

I'm not even sure they're alive.

I study them, look dead into the darkness of their eyes, examine their countenances for any spasm of muscles, signs which might indicate they're human, or at least were at one time. What seems like a small eternity passes. I find nothing.

Until one after another they begin to slide out of my sight, submerge themselves beneath the surface of this human sea. Just a faint ripple of movement, and they're gone. Do they know some secret means of escape? *I have to go!*

A scream swells in my lungs. I open my mouth to release it, but only a hoarse gasp escapes through my lips. The scream is caught tight in the back of my throat, a ball of bitter acids which knows I have no choice but to wait.

But it seems that one of the heads has returned. I recognize the abnormally long forehead and thin brittle lips, though I'm not sure it's the same guy because he isn't directly looking at me. Or anything at all for that matter, since his eyes are closed. But then I spot a second familiar face, watch as a third returns on the horizon, and there's no denying it: they're back. And oddly enough, with expressions of intense joy, eyes shut, corners of their mouths upturned in grins, lips shiny and red.

Another face returns with the same ecstatic look, and my blood rushes.

"They're on to something," my voice tells me in a dry whisper.

I hunch down, squat so low my forehead is smashed into the wet small of someone's back. Spirals of sharp odors fill my nostrils, pungent scents of ejaculation and excrement. My stomach knots in nausea, but I recognize the spoiled raspberry-colored swamp covering the cold marble floor and my sickness transforms into a tight uncomfortable craving. The red around their mouths. I've got to have it.

I force myself further down, strain and dip my hands wrist-deep into the muck, feel its warmth squish between the slats of my fingers. Then as if by instinct, my palms cup together and scoop the foreign substance into my mouth.

I feel euphoric as the mixture passes through my lips, slides down my throat, slick with mucus and blood, thick with scraps of nails and strands of hair. It's unbearably spicy, searing with an obscene sense of perfection running through my veins, streaming into my brain.

My head feels dangerously light as I stand back up, a high white noise, a strobe. My innards vibrate and my teeth clatter uncontrollably. The air glues a breath of mist to my nostrils. Then I glaze. Glaze over. Dust snows into me, snuffs out, thick as bonemeal. And then it's/then I'm fading. Almost immediately to the wants. To a greater, more desperate hunger.

Again and more strongly I'm aware of these bodies around me, only now I understand my link with them. Their mouths are my mouth; my mouth is theirs. Collectively we're nothing more than spare parts for a machine going through the stagnant motions of no incentive, no sense of absolution. Nothing but more. The need for more.

It hits me how long I've gone without another thought in my head. Not just during the bus ride, not just today, but yesterday, the day before, the week before, the month before. I can't remember the last time I actually felt like myself, like an actual person instead of a device that exists solely for the sake of its own mindless pleasure. Its indifferent ugliness. It astounds me. Disgusts me. Yet still I ache for more.

The expression, "It is never a good idea to offer the hand of help to one who needs it too badly," comes to me; these words a series of slaps that sting.

The scene is coming down around me and I stare at this ocean, thick and dark waves of wet heads rising and falling, slapping this mad existence somewhere against walls bricked and far away, way out there, stretching high with windows panelled cool green indigo gold aquamarine yellow, cellophaned mosaics behind which lie the wild rays of something bigger, life when it happens. As it happens. This can't be happening

My mind jumps its tracks again. Every program screened in my twenty-seven years is whizzing about. Memories. Scenes from sitcoms: *One Day at a Time, Three's Company, Strangers with Candy*. School photographs. Comic books. Am I sure this is real? Or that it's not?

Then my vision is washed with blue again, and I hear a metallic screeching. Axels grinding. The pressure of weight against break pads, rubber tires smearing streaks of graffiti onto the pavement.

Bright light. I fight to focus. Find that everything has changed. I'm back on the bus, back in my seat, but now there's a space next to me where once was a girl, an emptiness open wide across the vehicle as if bodies have been scooped up and dumped out.

I slide to the right, fill the aisle seat so I can see through the windows on either side, watch the pictures pass by.

The bus smooths to a halt, freezes on a frame with a street mime in a wrinkled white costume, tourists cramming themselves into a cable car, a billboard with a diapered baby, a mirrored high rise, images that snap the feel of San Francisco into place. Actually, I'm unfamiliar with this area of town, yet I feel a shift of weight in my feet and find myself standing as if I were waiting for this stop. All along. And then I'm moving forward.

I step into the world outside, the taste of something true in my mouth.

METAPHOR AND REMORSE

Gavin on my bed in my bedroom. He's hunched forward, his body in the shape of an F, hands at work on his compact mirror, boots dangling off the end of the mattress.

"So anyway, he's flying me down to L.A. on Thursday."

My CD player spins *ISDN*, the music of Future Sound of London.

"The computer animation geek. You know the one."

I shudder, don't speak. Attempt to act nonchalant. The clock moves its digital red teeth to 3:23.

"Said he wanted me to type something dirty — oh, and surprise, surprise could I do it in the nude, please — so I sat at his desk and wrote about microwave cupcakes while he jacked bird. Watched me from the futon. Didn't touch me once. I told you, right?"

He continues before I have a chance to answer. As if I don't already know who he's talking about.

"Only thing I said was, "I'm writing about sweet sticky stuff, man," and he shot his load. Hundred bucks. Didn't even take five minutes."

I correct the chalkboard of my mind: about whom he's speaking.

> *one time I tricked with a scat freak who referred to me as*
> *his "Sweet Lil' Rosebud" and had me squat over his face*
> *for almost two solid hours*

A retching sound escapes from Gavin as he swallows a laugh.

As if I could forget.

"Story is there's some lame play party going on this weekend in L.A. Plus that fetish club on Thursdays, Sin-A-Matic. Or is it Sin-A-

Matic that's on Saturday nights?"

His fingers freeze. So does he. I watch as he thinks about it a second, (mississippi one, mississippi two); then he shakes his head, resumes chopping the stash of speed on his mirror.

"Perversion or Sin-A-Matic or something like that," he says, speaking again, still neglecting to look at me. "Fuckin' whatever. Cyber chump wants to go, and he wants me to go with him. Personally, I'd rather sort my socks, but somehow I doubt that'll get me the seven hundred and fifty bucks. Not bad, huh? We both know I need it."

He tosses the razorblade aside. Silently, it lands on my sheets. He scoops a straw stub off the bed, curls his rough fingertips around it as if it were chopsticks — except he only has one, and it's hollow and much shorter, for dining with the nose.

"*We* need it," he says, one hand smoothing loose strands of his bleach-blond bangs behind an ear, other hand expertly positioning the straw tip inside his nostril.

His chest deflates as he exhales, his stomach stretching to a pooch. As he begins hunching forward, nosediving into his reflection, I move my gaze to the floor.

> *kinda raunch, I know but I really wasn't in a*
> *position where I could be picky since my last*
> *three johns had flaked out*

Patches of hardwood stained the color of milk chocolate peek from beneath a world of wadded-up socks and a dark coils of clothing, paperback books, stiff-bristled paintbrushes, shopping bags, cigarette butts.

> *I figure the reason business's been slow*
> *is 'cause of that new chicken who fucks for eighty dollars*

I pick a detail: colored notebooks in a loose stack, their edges pasteled, frayed. Crumpled papers dangle off the sides like handkerchiefs from the back pockets of Castro men.

I select a detail and try to reduce my world to this image. The soundtrack, FSOL's *Lifeforms* traveling through my speakers. Brashly interrupting them, those familiar noises again: a scratchy sucking sound like chat being vacuumed, the gurgle of a waterbottle fingerfuck, the wet sniffle as he hits his nostril with H_2O to cool the chemical singe.

> *One-legged Wayne's pranked his beeper a few times*
> *and punched in the S.T.D. Hotline number and the*
> *police station and stuff just for the hell of it*

My stomach's a mangled acidic mess, and I don't think my sight's all that great, either. The notebooks I've been staring at have bled together and begun to breathe. I've made a monster, it seems.

"Whoa."

I turn to him slowly, my head moving like a camera on a tripod. The instant his form returns to my frame of vision, I discover I can still make out the details of his features with remarkable clarity; even the pores of his skin are in focus, shiny indentations. His face is wrinkled and colored like asparagus. There are a few acne scars scattered about the landscape of his chin, marks which I find attractive in some strange and endearing way. However, most of my interest is concentrated studying his jawline, creating a sharp outline, convinced that the pads of my fingers would be sliced to the bone if I touched him.

"Yeaaah," Gavin moans, stretching the syllable and his neck, head back. "Fuckin' rad!"

My old man and his rockets. The meth's hit him, the sensation of sheer perfection spiraling up his throat and through his open mouth. Must be a good score. Gavin's so into it, the bed is writhing beneath us.

I run the hand of my glance over the expanse of his chest. He still can sizzle, whether or not I always want to admit it. I extend my arm, jonesing for the feel of his skin against mine when there's a tremor in my fingers, my wrist.

and I talked to the guys downtown to see if
I could get the skinny on him

"Is something wrong?" he asks and shifts his frame, moves closer. A hipbone juts forth, its sharp edge pressing against my thigh.

I grit a sharp cracking sound from my teeth trying to spit out an answer. The answer, any answer.

His eyes. I'm frozen by the sight of his eyes, eyes which used to glow, make me melt. Beautiful electric blue eyes that've gone foggy, their lustre dulled to cold smoky clouds, shadows beneath the arches of his brow that look deserted.

"Does it bug you that I'm doing the L.A. shag? I mean, aren't you glad that I've set up the cash flow?"

I can feel his eagerness as he waits.

"Sure," I say, my voice a garbled wet mass.

"Good." A beat. "Wait a sec. Sure it bothers you, or sure you're glad? Which one do you mean?"

so Chuck says his girlfriend Luta asked around and stuff
and turns out he's a SuperTweak who amps a sixteenth a day,
or some obscene amount

"Does it matter?" My voice is thick as the Dead Sea.

"Does it matter? Does it *matter?* he says, his voice wavering with the refrain.

Gavin's face registers signs of chemical burn as the second drip of meth drains down his tonsils. Eyes wide and webbed with crimson, he hacks a lumpish cough, swallows, clears his throat. Gulps water from the Calistoga bottle where fingers were seconds ago.

"Well, la-di-da! How 'bout your tuition, little princess? Does *it* matter?" He's bold with his fresh high, loaded.

"I thought you weren't going to throw that in my face again," I say, my cheeks beginning to heat with fury.

"Well," he prompts, "and *I* thought you weren't gonna be all weirded-out or Mr. Morality or whatever when I talk about hustling."

What I want to say − the fever of words and frustration I feel − throbs like an overtaxed metronome.

"It's just sex work," he tells me.

"Oh, thanks a lot. And after all this time of wondering what to call it −"

"Alright, Sheldon," he interrupts.

"No, it's not all right,'" I say. "It's not."

Gavin changes the mirror's position on the mattress, disregarding my comment.

"Listen," he announces, head bowed and tone solemn as he examines the microscopic details of his decision. "It's work. That's why they're called jobs: We're − I'm − not supposed to enjoy it."

"Sometimes you act like you do."

"Really?" he responds, his voice cool but stinging like a slap. "I wasn't sure whether or not you noticed, since spending my fuckbucks and playing student keeps you so preoccupied."

"You... asshole!"

> *which'd average out to be about a two trick minimum*
> *per day just to spot his works, if that's the case.*

"Asshole," he mocks. "So what do you think that makes you?"
What do I think.

"It's assholes like me that put shit like you in the world, baby."
What do I think? Dial-a-Cliché.

"Huh!" He grunts, stiffens his shoulders. "Really, what about you?

Just whadd'you think?"

What do I think? You don't want to know what I think, I think. You don't want to know what I've become.

Gavin slouches forward, seems to lose interest. Impetuously pokes at the mound of speed with his pinky nail. It looks like an opalescent bullet, like shimmery imperfect ammunition with glass shards for gunpowder. I study his reflection by way of the mirror as he cuts an uneven line, shoves the plastic stem into nostril, and inhales.

"C'mon. It's only till Sunday," he coaxes, his head back-turned, words tossed to the ceiling. Tangent to tangent: connect the dots.

Then leveling his gaze with mine, continuing, "Tell ya what. Think of it this way: when I return, I'll have made enough to cover your last payment."

But this is stuff I already know. Ought to be enough but isn't. By the irritation in his voice, sounds as if it's also not enough for Gavin.

"You're featurin' V.C.R.," I mutter, shuffling by the subject of my college tuition with a tip on his salt-rimmed nostrils.

Oblivious, he blinks; then his eyes lower. A flush of understanding passes over his face: *visible crystal residue.* He raises a fist to his nose, sniffs, shrugs his shoulders.

"Really though, what do you think that makes you?" he repeats, his voice booming.

"Does it matter?" Language is such a game. "Doesn't matter. Does it matter?" I dribble out words which might pass for an answer, study the way my mouth moves, feel the shapes it makes. The words continue to flow from me: "Doesn't matter. Doesn't. Doesn't."

"But I know what does," Gavin says. He thrusts his hips up, jeans down into a denim wad between his knees. A master of convenience, one swift unbroken movement and he's nude: pants loose enough on his lanky frame the buttons can be skipped, no skivvies beneath to remove.

"This. You can't even look at this; can't face all the things it stands for."

His dick.

He has half an erection, his penis dangling like a tree bent back by the wind. He takes my hand and places it around the trunk, anticipation obscenely audible on his breath as the CD reaches its end.

For a few seconds of the uncomfortable silence that follows, I study the hardening structure that was thrust at me as a dare or a consolation prize. The spongy purple head of his cock sprouts from my fist like a tulip and looks somewhat humorous. Gavin, however, emits a throaty growl as a signal this is no joke and slowly, slightly grinds his hips, inviting friction. I feel a surge of heat begin to rise from the soft, wrinkled flesh gathered at the base of his cock, tightening as it continues jumping to attention, ironing out the folds accordioned between my fingers.

I loosen my grip and push myself away. He does nothing in acknowledgment. Nothing more than replace my palm with his own, that is. He just lays there and strokes himself lazily and mumbles lyrics to a 10,000 Maniacs song.

"These / are / the days / to remember..." His voice is flat, completely stripped of emotion. Sounds like it needs about an eight ball of wonderstuff to put in flight.

"Should I put on something else?" I ask, interrupting him. I've practically made it across my obstacle course of a room and completed the task before he has a chance to respond.

it's not that the competition's a problem, really;
the problem's how the competition changes our clients

Positioned beside the stereo, I gravely watch him reanimate.

"Does it matter," he hisses, bony fingers slithering about himself as he stares at the ceiling.

I wish I could make his voice go away. I have the nervous urge to hum a tune, but my mouth is still; my lips, dry and tight.

My fingers clutch the plastic case of *Solutions for a Small Planet* by

Haujobb, from which I extract the CD and plop it into the player. Instantly, sampled noises and a heavy synthetic bass begin to fill the air.

"Another cool thing about the L.A. excursion is that you'll have some down time."

Down time. As opposed to now, when things are on the rise...

"You know, to study," he adds between tugs. His voice is bored and airy, like a porn star's.

Down to L.A. Going down to L.A. Going down.

"Great," I say. "Yeah, it's tough to keep up."

Paging Dr. Freud! No, that one wasn't obvious at all.

I wish I could shut up and stop thinking. There's a mental picture of Gavin squatting over a stranger's face, and I wonder when I'll be able to lose track of this imagined memory, if I'll even be able.

I can't, don't want to deal with this now. Also doubt I could handle more demolition work against my sinuses. There've been so many feelings stuffed up my nose, so many foreign chemicals and their hired pain, my tattered nostrils need to be put in traction.

"Will you do me a fix," I say, more an emotionless command than a question.

He nods, motioning to the forearm at work between his thighs. "Will you help me take care of this?"

I glance with cool contempt at the veiny rod he's palming. Take and give, the give-and-take.

"Sure," I say, staring him dead in the eyes from eight, ten feet away. Yet still close enough to make out my reflection in the swallowing blackness of his pupils.

I step towards him, towards those two wet shadows of myself – dark and familiar and disturbingly elusive – and suddenly experience the sensation of free falling. As if reality were perforated and somehow part of me slipped through.

The movement of my joints and bones compose a catastrophic ballet for which I can't help but feel forced backstage. First person shifts to some far compartment of my mind while I observe from third person, limbs that once were mine floundering, attempting to draw attention. Assert their independence.

I'm jolted out of my stupor by the image of Gavin below me on the mattress, the feeling of something below my foot.

Beneath my shoe is an empty bottle of Night Train, which a kick beneath the bed resolves quickly. Springs respond with a metallic screech when I sit on the mattress edge.

Gavin stares at me with a wet gleam of expectancy in his grayish-blue eyes. Steadfastly, I gaze back at him, at the reflection of me twice over.

"Uh-uh. Hit me first," I demand, shaking my head.

changes how much of their change they're willing to spend, you know, what they expect

Gavin extends an arm above his head, extracts the aluminum-cased First Aid kit from the end table with bored resentment. Stifling a yawn, he sits up, leans forward in a slight, half-determined lurch. Begins prepping the syringe without troubling to pull up his pants. His penis is a semi-erect glistening heap that just hangs there, sullen, waiting. The slit of his cockhead points at me like a vengeful eye.

I cross my legs, assume what's become the standard position. Eyes closed, my right hand squeezed into a fist, upper arm tourniqueted tight by my clamped left palm.

"That's right," Gavin whispers, his voice soft and low, warm like the seductive flow of blood where he's just registered. A shiver of goosebumps jump to attention along the nape of my neck as he directs me: "Perfect. Steady now; loosen up nice and easy..."

I loosen up the slack, cautiously release my grip.

Gavin's good, as usual. He's thumbed the plunger home and slid the apparatus from my skin sooner than I could notice. Eyes blink open to a flash: there's a fuzzy tingling and what feels like a tiny pinch; then the blazing contrast of meth as it hits me straight on.

Mmmmm I hear my body respond, guttural sounds of ecstacy gushing through my O-shaped mouth from the brilliant warm waves rolling throughout my limbs and breaking. A numbing stream of vitality coats my torso and dries my mucous membranes.

"Yum," Gavin says, copping what would be a contact high if he weren't already blazing and fumbling with his cock.

My body's chemically-altered chemistry is revved with a full tank of motivation, an active lie fueled by the most potent means available. Pupils gaping wide, I try to squint out the fluorescent yellow light which seems to have brightened, thickened, making everything look distorted. Blurred like a vision.

The lower portion of my body melts over the mattress's boundary and crumples on the carpet. Anchored by my elbows propped on the bed, I kneel in penitential silence before his cock.

I part my lips and press their smoothness at the base of the shaft, breathing heavily, inhaling the thick smell of desire and sweat. Exhaling slow and gentle, my breath a warm blanket I smooth over his dick and balls.

Gavin cups his palms around the back of my head.

"Oh yeah," he encourages. "Yeah, that's it. C'mon, do it, yeah!"

Moving in currents down his throbbing leanness, I paint lust pictures with my tongue – except this picture of us is missing lust. What used to be something special now feels just as routine as with the others, as anything else.

> *and how much they expect. I mean, who wants*
> *to work more and get paid less?*

Throat dry from the high riding me, Gavin continues riding my face. Against my fluttering eyelids, a submerged memory begins to surface with his increased desire and gag the spirits of my remembrance.

The wet forever of November wind swirls down San Francisco streets, whipping pedestrians' backs with thin icy ropes, slicing their chapped cheeks. In the rough drawling whisper of 1 a.m., it sweeps up garbage and dead leaves, wails stories of days gone by, the way things used to be. The night sky soaks up this shadow I've become, gets tinted a deeper, blacker hue of blue.

The painful need for stash sends me gerbiling to the Mission District, 17th and Albion.

A chipped silver gate flaps back and forth on its hinges, squeaking incomprehensible gossip and spitting flecks of spraypaint. I manage to dodge it, slink my way into the building's foyer.

Despite the faint white light filtered down through frosted glass, I notice the paper covering the walls is deeply faded and frayed. Polka dots in spots from water stains. Tiny baggies are scattered about the staircase and linoleum entryway, an array of colors and imprinted designs: patterns of hearts, spades, dollar signs, clubs, diamonds – even devilboys with dervish grins.

I trudge up three flights of stairs, then drastically slow my pace to grope and guess my way down a hallway that looks like it's closed. What lies ahead is dark as the belly of a cockroach, striped in one spot by a buttery yellow mark I shuffle towards: my target this muted light that creeps beneath B.D.D.B.'s door.

Tiptoeing and pausing a step short of the varnished particleboard, I recognize the muffled beat of house music. His cold, brittle laughter.

For some reason I'm plagued by an impulse to resist, a sudden urge to ditch this scene. But the reddish-orange throb of seratonin depletion that's snickering and pulsing through my temples leads my knuckles to the wood, gets them beating.

"Who's there?" a harsh, masculine voice inquires.

First I respond by his rap-rappity-rap-rap code; then I go clattering into his place like last week's leftovers.

"Ay, look who's come to pay us a visit!"

Big Daddy Drug Buddy's all about plural pronouns when he speaks, despite the fact that he lives alone – that is, excluding his vices and the building's rodents. He's leaning way back in his chair, reclining at his throne: legs crossed at the knee, feet propped up on his desk smothered by stacks of cash, his beeper, portable cellular, chunks of crystal, a long-barreled handgun. At arm's length, his necessary tools: a mirror, razor blade. A glass straw.

"Or just visiting to pay up?"

He laughs, and his open mouth reveals a cavernous brown wasteland, charred stumps with a glint of silver embedded somewhere in the bottom left corner. His skin is the color of butcher paper.

I smile feebly in response, trying hard to look like a good boy. Trying to keep up this game.

"Aw, come on in! Come in," he insists emphatically, nodding his head up and down so quickly his unmarked black baseball cap is a blur.

The air in the room is warm and stale, an oily bluish-gray curtain of cigarette and crack smoke hanging from the ceiling. Everything seems ghostly. Surreal and hollow, like objects in a dream. Dead, or maybe never alive at all.

"So, Sheldon. Whassup?"

The arrogant look in his dark eyes tells me he already knows. He uncrosses his legs, studying me for a reaction while he changes his position, his pose. Moves his right hand closer, rests it along his pants' waistband. Thumb tucked in the elastic, gnarled fingers tipped with split nails caress his crotch bulge.

His voice is suddenly low and serious. "Hey man, how's about me settin' you up with some a this?"

I hold my breath as my body rubbers, observing the unpleasant way his stomach strains the band of his pants.

"Wouldn't happen to want a little bump, would ya?" he taunts. "Huh?"

He motions to the mirror surface, a surly grin on his face. Ever so subtle about the extent to which he enjoys my discomfort.

"Brand new shipment in from Hawaii. Hella mothafuckin' nice ice, baby."

He begins chopping and dividing the rocky white pile. Laying it out.

"Gacks ya balls off real good, man." He swoops down his head and makes a line disappear through his straightshooter. Then he whistles low, swiftly strokes his cock through his clothes, as if I need a demonstration. "Nothin' like it."

The sight of the powder sends an avalanche of feelings piling up. Powerless at the sight, a yearning rages in my stomach, makes my testicles crawl.

"So how much were ya plannin' to spend tonight?"

I shrug my shoulders, shift my weight from shoe to shoe.

"Well," he persists. "How many dead presidents ya holdin'?"

"I dunno," I lie. Moist fingers dull the nervous jingle of the dollar thirty-five I have in my pocket.

"Aw, I'm sure we could work somethin' out. Maybe a swap. Ya know I'm a fan of the barter system," he sneers.

The way he looks at me – as if he wants me bound and gagged and brought to him on an appetizer platter – reminds me of my tongue, the most valuable currency I have to offer.

"Now, ya ain't forgot that hundred bucks I fronted last month as a loan. Have ya?"

I avert my gaze, humbly shake my head in opposition. *Nope, just like I haven't forgotten the difference between partying and peddling ass.*

"Good. So barter it is," he declares, eager to drive the meaning of "somethin'" home with a specificity that's first gear, upfront.

"Now, c'mon and tell Big Daddy Drug Buddy how much you love to suck on his pacifier."

Doesn't waste a second.

"Tell him how good you've been, how you wanna taste it naked, how he don't need no rubber on."

Instinctively, my jaw clamps shut, the thought of repeating those words sheer embarrassment.

"Aw, whassa matter, baby?" he mocks. "Crack got your tongue?"

The more I owe, the more extreme his requests go.

"Then again, guess not, or we wouldn't be here!" He laughs violently, mercilessly, erupting in spasms. Rewards himself with applause.

"So you're all grown up and don't like Big Daddy's pacifier no more. Well. I s'pose I'll just have to take this up with the Missuz."

A cruel, nasty smile curls up at the sides of his mouth.

"Zat whatcha want? Should I call me a conferenz wit' cha ol' bitch Gavin?"

"No!" Flames rush through my loins like the backlash of a blast heater. "No, of course not."

I swallow, force myself to untangle my tongue. Gain control.

"Big Daddy," I say, bleary-eyed, waiting for his reaction. "I - I love to suck on Big Daddy's pacifier."

His expression softens to that of his regular state of relaxed agitation, his wide face seamed with long deep trenches.

"I've been good, Big Daddy. Let me suck on your pacifier; please, Big Daddy, I'll make it good. Give it to me naked, I'll -"

"Won't ya just take a great big ol' suck on the devil's dick, now, son," he interrupts, snarling in excitement. "Time t' loosen up your mouth, get yourself spinnin' real good."

He shoves the glass pipe in my face, a sparkling load lit and melting, the dry smoke licking my eyes.

"Inhale," he demands, maneuvering the pipe closer, positioning it against my lips. "This is what you came for; get on with it!"

Getting on with it is exactly what he's doing: there's a heap of crumpled burgundy corduroy to the left of his socked feet from where B.D.D.B.'s already peeled off his shoes, his pants. I shiver as, in the lower half of my body, sexual arousal and disgust intertwine in heady confusion.

I breathe in a colorful high as he yanks, wrestles with my zipper. Then the carnival begins: my head fast and light, his eyes Tilt-a-Whirls.

Big Daddy Drug Buddy veers close-up to shotgun another hit. I shut my eyes and take the drugged smoke, vaguely noting when my white cotton boxer shorts slide off with a whisper. My legs buckle, and I follow them onto the cushiony ground, drop down on my knees.

I feel the vulnerability and the freedom of air tingling against my bare buns.

"Whoo-ee! Lookit that tight little pony pussy."

He snickers, leans forward in his chair for a closer look. Smacks his lips, slaps me across the ass.

"I'm gonna have t' take me a ride on this here carousel," he says. "Get my money's worth."

With a whoosh, my shirt comes off last.

Nothing new about this tale, he bends me back and rips pages from my spine. Alters impressions to my body's text through a chunk of my shoulder's without : bloody pieces of shorn skin breaking apart like paper towels, dissolving. Treading the lukewarm waters of his mouth.

I'm frozen with pain. Shocked.

Big Daddy Drug Buddy grabs me by the mane at the top of my neck. Pulls my head back, arches my back. Stares me deep into the eyes, his big black pupils glossy, quivering. Hungry for the next attraction.

"Dinner time," he whispers hoarsely.

Then calloused fingers rake through my hair, grip my hair by tugging two tight fistfuls of scalp to get a grip on my head. "Open wide," he commands. Impales me on the prick between his thick bowlegged thighs.

The musky chemical smell exuding from his pores and pubic hair singes the hair inside my nostrils and makes my eyes water. He pulls out with a sloppy slurping noise, stuffs it back in.

Big Daddy Drug Buddy drives his cock at his own rhythm, scooting forward to rock himself against me, push the full weight of his body in with each stroke.

I run a hand across his stomach sizzling like a hot griddle, zigzag a trail to his nipples. Graze against them. Eager to get him hotter, I let my fingers drift into the thicket of hair beneath his balls. He shudders with delight. Rearranges his weight, twists his legs back and upward to offer the hidden pink terrain of his anus. I diddle it as closely as I dare to get.

Until his heaving becomes deep breathing and then he leans all the way into me, exploding. His beeper goes off, an alarm clock signaling his orgasm I begin swallowing, dehydrated lips pulled tight over teeth, retching from the dick I keep pressed to the back of my throat.

It's a struggle to keep his salty poisons off my tastebuds.

He pushes me off him, and I collapse like exhaustion.

"You sure do love suckin' my dick, don'cha boy? Got me off good and fast," he says, zipping up his pants. "Figger that was worth at least a quarter bag."

Silent, I cover a blush and my body, limbs sliding back into clothes.

"Whatcha need per up for a party these days, anyway?" he asks, though I'm certain he's aware.

"A sixteenth," I say. The truth of my day-to-day sounds like sweaty desperation.

"Ah, that's right: a 'teener. Shit, it ain't been long since a quarter'd last ya an entire week! Gonna have to take me a raincheck on plowin' that ass."

Big Daddy Drug Buddy laughs a bronchitis wheeze and tells me I should start a club called 'Excessive and Habitual.' He checks the display of his pager going off again, fingers a seven digit call-back into his cellular phone.

"It's me," he informs the appliance. Tosses a chalky clear plastic ziplock in my direction without looking first. It smacks me across the collarbone, bounces into my lap.

I pocket it and bolt for the door, my fists in knots tight as my stomach, throbbing to punch a hole through the nightmare. This constant quest for more.

Gavin's spread out beneath me like an unfolded road map. I study the way he creases, survey the topography of his lithe frame which locks in excitement while I navigate with my tongue. High-pitched yet quiet, he squeals when I increase the rhythm, slide my open lips down his cock bone and up the middle vein. Flick the fat tip. Rub it back and forth along the cordlike underside.

I play with him. Admire his shoulders curling back into the bedspread, the tendon in his neck raised tight as a bowstring.

Then he comes, his body cracking like a licorice whip. The rhythm of his thrusts reaches a crescendo and the first wad blasts against the roof of my mouth. It's followed by a stream of sticky whelps, an exclamation point that slides into my stomach.

Afterward, in the absence of tangled limbs and heavy breathing, he doesn't dress.

I look to the sharp-tipped teeth of clock chattering out 3:47 a.m. They tell me nothing else.

There's a flash of something square-shaped and silver, a wobbly movement which comes into focus: the mirror. I guide it towards me, decide to check my face as a reminder of my identity. But what I see feels like I'm gazing down at an open-casket funeral. This face is old and twisted, tousled black hair resembling worn typewriter ribbons.

Gavin parts his lips, balances a cigarette between them. Returns my stare with a look as void of expression as he is of clothes.

I'd think by now he'd know what I do, what I've done, just by looking at me. Yet he doesn't. Doesn't seem to notice anything at all.

Didn't even try to remove my shirt concealing evidence of the scab burning fresh on my shoulder blade, its bloody moisture clinging to the cotton in a silhouette. I want nothing but the best for the both of us.

There are lots of places to hide things, when and if a person wants.

The mirror - like Gavin, like me, this busy bloodstreamed room, the world - one giant cramped image. A framework attempting to contain what it can never possess.

"So, when is it you're supposed to ride the skies?"

The world which surfaces through these words is wide and far away and doesn't touch him at all.

"Huh?"

"Your flight?" Quite large, this task of small talk. I translate: "What time is it?"

"Like eleven or something. Around noon. Why?"

"Just wondered."

"Oh..." His voice trails off, gets inhaled with a drag of his cigarette.

"I mean, is CyberChump giving you a lift, or do you need me to call a shuttle?"

"Cyber's got it covered," he says, a smile beginning to steal its way across his face. "But thanks."

how the competition changes

I cock my jaw in a noncommittal gesture of 'you're welcome,' and he scoots closer, closes the distance between us by hoisting himself on top of me, wrapping his wiry arms around my neck in a forced hug. I sigh silently; then I take a deep breath and hold it in, attempting to dodge the stickiness of his shrivelled dick against my shirt.

Sensing heat, my glance meets Gavin's cigarette cherry dangling mere inches from my face. Serpentine and tipped bright red, the image threatens me, ignites my defenses. I shove him off me onto the crumpled bed we share, the words "Watch it, spaz!" blurting out.

"God, *sorry*," he says, the words leaking out like wilted exasperation. His jaw drops with his gaze, flicks the ash in his palm for added effect.

A Drama Queen O.D. veteran, I pretend not to notice. Try to keep the course of conversation flowing while I can.

"So you don't need a ride. Well, don't *you* just float like a dandelion puff wherever the wind takes you?" I joke, though it doesn't turn out sounding much like that. Now with a nerdier, more exaggerated inflection, "What'd he do, e-mail you the vital stats?"

"Faxed it, sweetie." He senses my sarcasm and works his face into a bent and disarming grimace. "Absofuckinlutely."

"Three nights, four days," I say, idly staring off into nothingness., into wide open white space. "And just the two of you?"

"Except for the play party, yeah."

"Maximum yuppie torture. Shit! What're you gonna talk about, iced cappucino and futons?"

"Sure." He shrugs it off. "Why not?"

From the floor he grabs a McDonald's carton still housing a few soggy french fries. Dabs out his cigarette.

"No, really."

"Really," he blinks, says in a thin, casual voice. "Who cares what we talk about? I don't think of him as a person, Sheldon. He's just another john. Another slave to my dick. Another employer. We've been through this before."

Another slave to his dick.

the both of us

"I give him a mouthful; he gives me enough dough to fill my pockets, or to find a new connect. Then I go."

"Right. You're right," I chant, wondering how much more of this life I can take before my skin splits at the seams. "Who cares?"

The fluorescent light from the bulb in the ceiling seems to make the room go grainy like a bad photograph. In the haze beginning to creep into the edges of my vision, I watch him suck his Benson and Hedges all the way to the filter.

Gavin tilts his head in my direction to check what my silence is all about. "So, hey. You holdin'?"

It takes a moment for his words to register, topic to sink in.

Drugs. Talk about surprise, surprise.

"Dry."

A beat, and then he asks again. "Nothin', man?"

"What, misplace your supply or somethin'?" I lift the mirror, flash both sides of it at him while – with my other hand – I stroke its absence on the sheet.

"Ladies and gentlemen, observe: nothin' up my sleeve," I smirk. With my index finger, swirl a scooping motion around inside the t-shirt sleeve. "Emphasis on nothin'."

"Okay smart ass, I think I get it. Nothing. Nada."

"Neat-o," I say, the mirror a stage I've placed between us, my voice like I'm talking into a dead mic.

He glances at the reflecting glass, at me. "Yeah. Neat-o. So, you have a full schedule today at school?"

"Uh-huh," I lie, suddenly panicked because I don't know what day it's become, can't remember what yesterday was.

"Couple lectures, a workshop. Oh yeah, and a class presentation this after–" I stammer, eagerly awaiting Gavin's response. My panic is a replica, a wax doll. What rush of blood, what life is there in fear of getting caught if no one's looking at all?

"Break a leg. This should help," Gavin says, the tone of his words too bored to believe in themselves, too mechanical to comprehend the humorous combination in which he recited them. He offers me a present – what he calls a gift, the gram he and I've been dipping from – and I don't think I've ever worked as hard for anything in my life that I don't even want.

changes

Doesn't life truly imitate art. As a loner and a liar and a plagiarist, I fit right in.

what they expect

There's so much I should say, so many things I should tell him, but in the end I tell him nothing.

I cut a line and my losses, and I light a cigarette.

THE DREAMING REAL

Spencer,

Wednesday night and I just got in from the gym, which was an incredibly humbling experience, as always. I had a couple of movies to return, so I went to the Hollywood branch (branch? That can't be right — sounds like a bank), which is quite the bright lights buffed body experience compared to the pastel-neon early '80s hangover location downtown. At any rate, one of this year's (millennium's) resolutions is for me to shake off as much of this post-speed fat as possible. That and continued sobriety and attempting to clean up the wreckage of my past, pardon the cliché.

Which is where you come in, buddy boy. Not as a cliché, but I'm sure you already guessed that. Oh Spencer, my former sidekick, boyfriend, partner in crime: where do I even begin?

You're in Austin, Texas, doing whatever it is you're doing, and I'm in (Hel)L.A., that Babylon-on-the-Pacific with the bad reputation I'd heard so much about and now think of as home. Funny that this is the place I threw my belongings in a U-Haul to escape to, blazing out of S.F. on yet another speed relapse, ignoring all the warnings that this is a "soulless town that'd suck me dry" and other histrionic rhetoric. And funnier still that this smoggy city stretched out like a surreal virus is where I've moved and am moving forward.

The most monumental change being the absence of drugs. Now that I'm over a year down the sobriety road, on the water wagon, off the sauce, et cetera — now and especially now that I've had some time and distance to process my involvement with intoxicants and their involvement with our involvement with each other, do I realize that everything of absolutely everything that was my everything was drugs drugs drugs drugs drugs.

And what an exhausted topic it is. How predictable the equation of chemically-induced euphoria leads to wondering if maybe this time it'll be better, if maybe it just went wrong those other times leads to careening dangerously from catastrophe to catastrophe. No new tale to tell, no? Drugs are Bad. Speed Kills. Dope Sucks. We know we know we know....

Yet here I am. And as much as I'd rather click delete and click on some cable t.v., as much as I'd rather clip my toenails, sort my socks or do just about anything other than sort through this mess, here I am. Here I am because I know I have to be. Here I am because I know that no matter how many times the story's been told, no matter what changes in location, special effects or fancy lighting, the difference this time, the difference for me, is that this story is mine.

When the truth of this matter is that I wouldn't change a thing about my story. (I would, however, cease sounding like a Carly Simon song. What am I gonna spout out next, that I "haven't got time for the pain"?) Natch, what I've been through has made me who I am today and I've been enlightened through my experiences and now I'm higher-powered and all those other bumper-sticker slogans that make rainbows sprout from the behind and the general population go *yawn*.

But it's true. That those are platitudes — and that if I could do it all again, I would, of course. It'd be a helluva lot more fun than sitting here at home in Converse tennis shoes, pecking away at my powerbook, trying to give some closure to you and the night and the madness.

I'm doing it now because I *choose* to. That's 'choose' in italics not just for emphasis but also for the purpose of foreshadowing. Y'see, when I first got sober — after I holed away at Mom and Dad's for 18 days of head-banging carpet-matting teeth-clenching anxiety attack withdrawals — after I called *that* sobriety, even though I was spiking Coke cans with

Jack Daniels at 10 a.m. and washing down Valium and Klonipin as my daily vitamins and finishing the whole mix off with a Vanilla Stoli chaser – and after I continued this newfound sobriety by inhaling a few mounds of coke so I could make it through the day (cause of course *that* didn't count! It was only *coke*. Like *crystal-lite*. Haven't you heard? *Nobody* ever gets addicted to cocaine) – yes, after all the rationalizations and denial and boundaries that my "best thinking" consistently proved me to cross, I found myself broke and broken and ashamed, shooting up crank in the living room of a MacArthur Park apartment inhabited by Satanists that were friends of my newfound "friend" who was an ex-stripper turned prostitute with a Dilaudid habit which of course didn't count either because at least she isn't shooting tar anymore but did I think I could find a vein because all of hers are shot but she'd really like to shoot speed and about 4 in the morning as I dusted off my share of a sixteenth and I looked around the room with its charming coffin bookcase, human skull candle and inverted pentagram decor and its glamorous hosts playing checkers with themselves and huffing on glass pipes, then and finally then it dawned on me that what I really needed to look at was myself, because that was unquestionably not sobriety. The gig was up. I wasn't fooling anyone anymore, most of all myself. It was time to check out that program – you know the one. The Program.

And that was the last time I used. That night before my first meeting was the last time I used. It was the 2nd of January, and I sat sobbing in Roman's room, tears spilling all over his technicolored fun-fur landscape of a bed as I waited on Erin – the only semi-anonymous successfully recovering alcoholic-addict I knew of in the city of Angels – to return my page. She did, and she told me where to go and I did.

The meeting was in the back of a Sunset café. I didn't have the foggiest what to expect. A professor/mentor of mine had taken me to a recovery group once up in S.F., but since I was still amped-up and under the auspices that I could "control my problem" at that juncture in my story, it wasn't exactly a positive experience. Not that it was a negative experience — it just was one of those I-Barely-Remember-Experiencing-It experiences. A 12-Step placard on the wall and lots of beefy Castro dudes sporting t-shirts so tight, they could've been stolen from a Jr. High basketball team; I recall little more.

As Roman helped direct me on the trek from Hollywood to Silver Lake (bright-lighted and honked at by nearly every other car on the road as I drove dangerously below the boulevard speed limit) for some reason I envisioned being surrounded by middle-aged middle-of-the-road alcoholic types at the meeting. Ogilvie-permed beauties huffing long brown-paper-bag cigarettes, wheezing frosty pink lipglossed tales of bingeing on Boons Farm while hubby Bubba worked the factory swing shift. Where I got that I don't know. Did Jerry Springer and the shallow end of the gene pool dip into my collective unconscious or has any "_.A." (fill in the blank) group generally and intimately been associated with white trash?

Whatever the case, I had decided that this would be my peer group. My salvation. Even if in exchange I'd be completely bereft of any coolness whatsoever, it'd be a fair trade. I had, after all, exhausted all other options. I couldn't live with the paranoia, the pain and voices and people rattling about in my skull, so I'd hang with the homemakers.

Ha. What I found instead was a room full of people to whom I could relate. Young people, hip people – some of whom I already was acquainted: the doorgirl from a club I frequented, a makeup artist who'd spackled me for a fashion show, a hairdresser who'd straightened my 'fro once. People who shared stories of past existences not unlike what then was still my present. But they had made it out. They didn't have to tell me; it was obvious. While I was a shaky, gravy-skinned mess hunkered down in the corner, they laughed and interacted around me. They hugged, greeted each other like old friends. And – as Gaylord as I know it sounds – light. So many of them seemed to have light in their eyes and a lightness about them.

Ahem... I'm getting too Amy Grant here. The long and short of it is

I identified as a newcomer, a few of the girls talked to me – general stuff, good to see you here, hi my name is – and one of the guys. The fellow was what I think of as a Godshot, now, in retrospect. It was after the meeting, and Roman and I were walking towards my car, when my nervousness waned and I realized I had to pee. Badly. I glanced back at the café but couldn't fathom my return: everyone had spilled out onto the sidewalk, smoking and socializing and blocking the entrance. I was gripped with fear. I was too intimidated to face these people again, these Life-is-Great/I'm-at-Peacers, but was even more afraid of being busted if I just whipped it out and took a whiz there between parked cars or behind a garbage can.

Fortunately I handed Roman my keys and felt compelled to brave my way back to the café. And the guy who stepped through the bathroom door a split second before me is who kept me coming back again. No, not like that; get your mind out of the cable telly! What I mean is, after he took care of his business, he introduced himself to me and basically introduced me to the program. He gave me the gist of how it works: one addict helping another, what I should do and where I should go.

He told me about sponsorship, a term I'd only heard Sharon Stone toss around in *Casino* and in reference to financial backing. This kind of sponsor was sort of like an emotional and spiritual backer, he explained. Someone who could share their experience, strength and wisdom on the whole sobriety trip. Someone who would be there when questions or cravings reared their nocturnal heads and sucked with sharp fangs. The sooner I could get a sponsor, the better, he suggested – which didn't sound like a bad idea.

He was the last person I spoke with that night (excluding Roman, who got a few grunts and light whimpering before I collapsed in bed) and the first person I encountered when I went with Erin to a meeting the following morning. We talked again and that was when I asked him if he'd be my sponsor. Circa _.A. (since I hadn't committed which one I was yet), not *Casino* – although sobriety's a gamble. Eww... hiss hiss boo, that one was absolutely odious, but I just couldn't resist....

So anyway, instead of what I first called sobriety – that Valley of the Dolls-induced stint with alcohol maintenance – but rather when I felt I had "signed up" and really got sober, I was like a froth-mouthed foot-washing baptist televangelist, eager to spread the word. Share the miracle. As if I had to, as if I had no choice. A few of my friends humored me – or at least made meager attempts – but basically the end result was that my phone rang a lot less frequently.

Of the old gang, Bob – who actually writes her name as ★BOB★ – is the only other one to shun pollutants, and she even beat me to it by a good year and a half. Who would've ever thought... ★BOB,★ the first female female-impersonator I ever encountered and one of the most insanely creative people on the planet; ★BOB,★ who did a four-year extensive couchsurf tour of San Francisco because all her cash went to her wigs and into her nose; ★BOB,★ who let me videotape her attacking strangers on the street with a rolled-up newspaper and smoking crack in my bathtub just so we could deem it art and have it displayed on 20 video monitors the opening night of Vice?

And you know what? She's just as much a kook as ever. She gets flown out to L.A. frequently as a hostess for Suzanne Bartsch and for club performances, and hanging out with her is comparable to the whirlwind it used to be. There's just no aftermath. Her last trip in town, we strolled up and down Hollywood Boulevard in search of feathery dangly glamorous stripper gear. She scored some pink sequin star-shaped pasties, while I entertained myself trying on six-inch platformless fetish heels and wobbling around Frederick's like an epileptic drag queen, moaning, "I just wanna be *loved*, Mary!"

Next I took her by the Angelyne Management Company office so she could peruse new merchandise of the Enchantress herself; then we went on a billboard tour about town and ended up sipping Vanilla Marble espresso sundae shake thingys at this Melrose café where we could windowshop hot punk rock boys off the street. That night I carried her (s)exercise mat for her and beautiful Brant and I served as escorts for her Topless-Aerobics-While-Eating-Cheeseburgers-in-Six-Inch-Heels-to-AC/DC performance. An absolute riot; the crowd went *crazy*. The next night, she did her "Jugs for Jesus" gig at club Cherry, where she gets all Post-Op Non-Stop Psycho Televangelist about it and pulls audience members up on stage and exorcise/exercises their demons and devils away by plopping her God-given 44Fs atop their heads. Then the following night we caused a ruckus at Sin-A-Matic when ★BOB★ was unaware of the Six-Feet-Away-From-Exposed-Nipples-in-L.A. cabaret venue law (which I was as well, until that eve) and peeled off her bikini, sprayed whipped creme from a can all over her chest and topped (har har) it off with cherries to the tune of "Cherry Pie" by Warrant or some Aqua-Cement-in-Yr-'Fro/Metal-Up-Yr-Ass, Man band from the '80s and pulled me up on stage and smashed my face in it, smothering me in cleavage and a sloppy pink cherry juice lather until Security yanked me off the stage. Ah, the scandal! And all without huffing hot rails off my kitchen stove, all sans salvation inhaled from a glassine baggie. All the insanity, none of the chemical dependency. I love it lurve it I love it!

Perhaps sobriety's just a thrill for the mentally ill. (Ew... now I'm rhyming! and *without* missing sleep for a week.) Whatever the case, I've come to terms with the fact that it isn't for everybody. Sobriety, that is. Missing sleep for a week isn't for *anybody*, but that's a given.

Yes, this is an attempt to make amends. I repeat: SOBRIETY IS NOT FOR EVERYONE. That's a really difficult one. Difficult because I don't want it to be true. Difficult because it is. Difficult because in your case I'm not sure it is, but the point is that it's your case − not mine.

Sure, even if you're still using and call me only when you're in the grip of the grape, slurring words and spilling out emotions you later claim to not remember or claim you don't claim them as your own. Sure, even if you swallow more tavern tokens than Betty Ford and more often than not have to be put to bed with a shovel. Sure, even if you've surfed through courtrooms, jails and Christian rehabs. Or surer still if you've spent a month-and-a-half skitting cross-country via Greyhound bus and Amtrak train because you were (or at least I was) convinced that the Mafia or some "Kill a Queer for Christ" extremist group (read: mass methamphetamine-induced paranoia) was hot on your trail. Sure, if you've ever been 5150ed by the Psychiatric Evaluation Team (no thanks to you and Rachael. Just because I was flipping my wig, flinging dishes and threatening to kill myself didn't mean I was actually SUICIDAL, guys! Jeez!), had 911 on your phone's auto-redial, a VIP card at the psych ward – these are pretty good signs that your life is unmanageable.

But who am I to judge? Let's hear it for rhetorical questions. I'm really struggling with that one. Really struggling with that. When I see someone headed where I've already gone, when I see someone heading somewhere which potentially could be worse, which could very well be a place from which she/he/it/shit couldn't, can't return, I want to get involved. Interrupt. Give the answer, the Answers nobody wants to hear. So of course when she/he/it/shit thumbs the nose, stiffens the shoulders, gives me the cold one, I don't want to hear it; I don't want to hear how it's different for them, or they've already got everything under control or it isn't any of my business.

Which it isn't. It isn't, and it's just about as inappropriate as chewing with my mouth open. It isn't, and it's as socially graceful as picking my teeth with my fingernails after inhaling a box of KFC.

It isn't, though it is. It's my business just so long as I share my experience, show where I went and what ambulatory madness I lived and how amazing it is that I lived through it, rather than tell anybody else what's right for him. Her. Them. *You.* That's right: for you, I apologize for being all huffy and prissy and forceful and self-righteous the last time you came to visit, the last time we spoke on the phone, the last time and all the other times that I was short and snappy over you having a drink or having a blast or getting blasted. I'm sorry. I'm sorry and I'm rambling, and I'm sorry.

Your life is yours, and your decisions are yours to make. (and now for something else you've totally never heard, right?) But I should stop the second person, cease the finger-pointing and turn this back to me. As if this is all about me. *As if.* Though when I started using, I really thought it was.

I started doing drugs as a declaration of my own independence, my quest for self-discovery. I became an illicit-substance enthusiast because it was my own body and my own decision. Laws were silly and dropping or popping or huffing or snorting or slamming was nobody's business but my own. It was my right to choose; it was my own choice.

And it was. But when I couldn't get out of bed without inhaling a colossus-sized line which then led to not breaking my coma until Jade or Derek or Dharma the Tang Lady (I still can't believe she ran that stuff up) or someone, *anyone,* administered a shot, it was no longer a choice. And when I was selling my CD collection, clothing and books in secondhand Haight Street shops or on the street just so I could cover the next day or the next dose and the next dose, it was no longer a choice. And when I overdosed, defecating and projectile-vomiting a la Linda Blair split-pea soup all over Brandon's studio and myself, and Hannah and Shawni and Lynda had to gather up garbage bags and line the back of Lynda's father's car so they could drop me at UCSF, yet still when they released me from the hospital 16 hours later after pumping me full of saline solution and sedatives and waiting till my heartbeat slowed (!) to 140 BPM and told me I was lucky to still be alive and I had to go home and celebrate with the remainder of a gram I'd hidden inside a Death in June (ironically enough) album cover, it was no longer a choice.

And when I blazed through $18,500-a-year's worth of student loan money, maxed out credit cards with cash advances, and squandered any and all semblance of my life's savings on drugs, just because I no longer knew how to live without drugs, because I couldn't take a shower do my laundry walk to the grocery store unless I'd copped and fixed my drugs, it was no longer a choice. And when I had to lie, to start hiding my intake from drug buddies and my dealers because I was out of control and in fear of being cut off, it was no longer a choice. And when I lost apartments, and when I lost lifelong friends, and when I saw an 18-year-old kid overdose and die in front of me, blood seeping from his nose in a sinister trickle and foam white and bubbly like bath suds spewing through his pale blue lips and I wouldn't even dial 911, couldn't think of anything other than bolting with Tobi and her baby from that Fox Plaza apartment and down Market Street because I was high, gacked out of my gourd and emotionally unavailable and unaware of what might happen to me if I were implicated, it was no longer a choice.

And when I sucked off my dealer for a quarter of dope, and when I volunteered my right shoulder to friends/fiends/photographers as a chopping block, having them cut Xs with an Xacto knife so I could gush crimson see something feel prove to myself that I was still human, and when I had no clue how to spell reality let alone provide a definition, it was no longer a choice.

Alright, you get the idea; I'm sure. But about this reality thing, there's something I have to clarify. In the beginning, my infatuation with speed wasn't so much that I wanted reality dismissed. Au contraire, I claimed that I wanted to experience more of it, burn right through the pinprick of existence, live life fasterharderdeeperwetterbetter. And I did – back when it worked, I really did – and it was really real, even if it really wasn't.

I had a grasp on the world, even if that grasp was on a syringe or a straw, even and especially if that world existed only for me. A needle, a spoon, a vein. And all my neurotic manifestations.

These days I'm interested in checking out the world around me. Looking outward, not limiting my scope. I'm attempting to be a part of it rather than an occasional visitor. A dazed and disgusted tourist. After years of tunnel-vision, hiding beneath blanket statements like the world is full of shit, shitty people eager to take what they can and roll you over, yakkety schmack, trying to find a place, my place on the planet, is a nice change of scenery. It's also a relief to no longer be weighed down with resentments.

Let me give the asterisk, the fine print, the disclaimer here: I'm not all happy-go-lucky tree-huggin' bark-snortin' Visualize World Peace whirled peas to Save the Children Sally Struthers late-night infomercial action about it. I don't give change by the handful to toothless panhandlers outside 7-11; I'm not interested in changing the planet – or much more than my hair color(s) or outfit, actually. That big and bold campaign stuff's beyond me.

But the little things aren't. Like actually listening when someone's speaking to me, instead of thinking of what I can/could/should say next, or what/whom I should be doing instead. Giving a ride, going to coffee with a new player in this whole sobriety game. Or babysitting someone through a rapid detox – not for bonus points, sans any gold star on my forehead. Simply because it makes me feel better. For no agenda other than I know it's the right thing to do.

And that's what helps me notice the blessings, the right things in my life and in living and in this living breathing macrocosm, instead of only the wrongs. The shouldn't haves. The should've beens. But rather the is and are's.

Like my family, my mom and dad who have been more patient and supportive and caring than I could've imagined. My mom and dad, who I thought would never understand me, and couldn't as long as I didn't give them the chance to. The chance to know what my problems were, the chance to help. The chance to know where I'm coming from, who I really am.

And who I am today is a person who's really here. Here and attempting to be aware of the present, rather than being afraid I was so damaged and had done so much damage that I was composed only of past and no future.

Last week I flew back to Arkansas for my grandma's funeral, and I'm so grateful I was able to be present. Not just physically there, but mentally there as well: present and able to interact, to be in the moment. To feel –

my emotions, emotions for the passing of the woman who baked sugar cookies for me when my mom was in the hospital, for the woman who held me on her lap and sang to me in my high-strung/pre-strung-out formative years. To feel and be considerate of others' feelings: my mom on the death of her mom, my uncle, aunts.

This must be sheer *fromage* to you, baby. But if growth beyond the I-Hate-You-First-and-More/I-Don't-Need-Nobody/I-Am-The-Lone-Wolf code is cheezy, make mine a fondue. Heh heh. Marq-E Modell, this cracked-out drag queen in S.F., said it best: "It's so hard being Goth. You have to have a bad time everywhere." I nearly lost my fake fangs over that one (*Thank Groin* I never owned any! Talk about cheeseballs flying into the room! Oops, wait though... there *was* that one photo shoot. Color me vicious pink with embarrassment...). Not that being Goth is necessarily having a bad time, nor that feeling bad(ly) is a lack of emotion – but anything that's that sedentary/constant/void of ebb and flow is lacking, the way I see it. But here I go with the hasty generalizations. Being an active addict really had nothing to do with being a gloom cookie; I just glamorized the sorrow and feeding my chemical needs guaranteed I stayed there.

I'm not really sure where I'm going with this. Help. Ah yeah, *help* — My life has become more complete through the realization that I can't handle it on my own. Once I surrendered, once I gave up my personal battle to quit, once I accepted the fact that I, alone and unaided, couldn't stop drinking and using, a tremendous burden was lifted. All that isolatory madness – all that secret guilt and shame – was released. I may have started out as a substance enthusiast, but underneath, I knew it was wrong. All wrong. All along.

Granted, I'm not saying that today I'm miraculously halo-blessed and right. That's not really the issue. What I'm trying to do through this letter is let you know that I love and appreciate you. Acknowledge that I was often a raging, hypercritical, impatient, possessive asshole and apologize for it. But I've realized something while writing this. This is also an apology to myself.

Y'see, nonchalantly hammering out a letter is a welcome respite from my self-conscious, ultra-edited attempts at making sense of things through any other forms of writing. Trying to tell my story through the guise of another's voice and skin; translating my emotions into precise diction or a strict poetic form. It's not the same, nowhere near the same. It's too much of a responsibility. More pressure than I can fathom. Probably because I've yet to figure everything out, and I don't particularly want to. I suppose that's my greatest fear about growing old: ripening into a sanctimonious tight-lipped queen who thinks (s)he has all the answers. That's the real death-in-life: having nothing left to learn. And for the first time in a long time, I want to live.

Living means that I've learned how to answer the phone rather than cower in fear over whom it might be. How to clean my room and do the things that normal (read: adjusted) people do.

I've learned an entirely new set of values – honesty, patience, openness with my family, the importance of doing constructive acts without expecting anything in return – and I'm working on personality rehabilitation. Taking care of the internal environment and letting the external environment take care of itself. Like with friends. When the phone rings, it's because someone wants to have a conversation, not some sketchoid who wants to score or have me hook him up with a connection. And trust. I'm learning how to trust.

Living means I'm learning what genuine happiness is. As well as what it isn't. When I was using, it wasn't long before I got to the point that I didn't enjoy anything anymore, except for the first few minutes right after a fix. And then came the crash, the crash came quicker and always more quickly, leaving me edgy, uncomfortable in my own skin, dangerously depressed and restless. Depressed and desperate for something else, for some other way, but unaware what to do to get there, depressed and desperate for more out of life but living for nothing but another fix.

There's great peace in the fact that I don't have to live the way I was living ever again. And no matter what problems may come my way, I don't have to go through them alone. I can help as well as get helped, which is an amazing experience.

Much like the freedom of choosing, of choice. I wish I knew how to fill in the margin; I wish I could explain how I regained the capacity to choose. I realize there's a gap the size of David Letterman's space-endowed choppers in my story. It's just that it's a lot like explaining how to walk. Sure, there's lots of tumbles and trial and error, but it's blurry once our feet are in motion. I mean, it hasn't been long since all I could do was chain-watch rental videos, chow on pizza deliveries and sporadically roll out of bed and make it to a meeting. But I made it and that's why the 24-hours-at-a-time thing has become personal, has this value. Somehow the 24-hour increments have piled up, and somehow I've regained the attention span to read and the ability to write and the ethic to work. And the capacity to love. I love that I'm able to love. It's a dominion, a state of being I didn't have to enter, it entered me – though I'm not sure how. That sounds goober, huh? So very Behold-the-White-Light fuzzy teddy bears and unicorns. So I'll shut up.

So my story has a happy ending, but not of the conventional kind. I didn't get sober and suddenly get whisked away into the cookie-cutter perfect relationship, job and apartment. In fact, I should have a bumper sticker on my Mazda that says *My Other Car Went Up My Nose.* My attempts at exploring the not-so-wide world of drug-free homosexual dating were nothing short of disastrously humorous. I'm in debt to the tune of about 100,000 smackeroos, a tune I assume is pretty much on endless repeat due to my current source of employment, which at best is a low-income experiment in humility. Then there's my second job: working for Angelyne. Who would've ever thought that I'd be personal assistant to a Hollywood icon and the world's reigning Billboard Queen? How's that for fuckin' GLAMOROUS. (Behold the brave lack of question mark! Apropos, though – and with scarcely a trace of naughty high-bitch wit.)

I like to tell people we met because my hair matched her Corvette, and although it's true that my coiff was Fudge Flamingo Pink, the truth of the matter is I made her acquaintance when I interviewed her for *Permission* at the Hotel Roosevelt. We giggled over coffee and crabcakes and got along great. Then the next week we met for iced Mochas at the Bourgeois Pig; I confessed to her that I had a burning desire to start a Kult ov thee Angelyne, whose upper eschelons would be crowned TelevAngelynists, and our friendship was pretty much sealed in silicone.

The first work assignment I did for her was hooking her up with a Pink Millennium Madness show at Bryan's club, Cherry. All the personal assistant stuff came once she signed the dotted line: it was my duty to see to it that she had (I'll never forget this) 5 pepperoni pizzas, 3 pitchers of Shirley Temples, 13 brownies with whipped creme, 44 helium-filled balloons in 3 shades of pink tied with red curling ribbon, 22 red roses, 8 Birds of Paradise, 3 flashlights and one leopard-print chaise lounge. All of these for good luck, and all of this just for her to lip sync one song. I SHIT YOU NUNCA, BABY. Since then I've assisted her by negotiating talk show appearances, escorting her to papparazzi-buzzed parties, and helping out with gallery bookings for her art (she's neon-painted 70 large canvasses to date – all of them self-portraits, natch). Needless to say, the Lady is quite a study in fabulosity, as is my new existence. Nothing makes me happier, until I change my mind. Heh. That's the true happiness in this end, my beginning. I'm learning what choices *really* are.

Basically, it all boils down to this: I've come to terms with the fact that I will always love foofy cocktails, whiskey shots in crimson-lit smoky dives, massive shots of methamphetamine. That searing sense of perfection, the prospect of a life of pure sensation: there's nothing like it. Conversely, there's nothing like the freedom of knowing that I could go out and get loaded this very second, but I opt not to because it just doesn't work for me anymore. The chemical lie is no longer worth the consequences.

Which is why now, dear chum, I choose to tuck myself in bed. It's pushing 5 a.m. and I completely lost time in the hours of this, the ours of this. This letter that I don't know if, doubt I'm ever going to send you.

The air outside is a palette ranging from slate gray to semitransparent roses and pinks, fluffy and disposable like tissue. It's a dawn's dream. The dawning of another day.

Call me Oprah and I'll kill ya.

Love and Best,

Clint